Fish in Paneer Soup

Fish in Paneer Soup

Deep Ghatak

Rupa . Co

Published 2011 by
Rupa Publications India Pvt. Ltd.
7/16, Ansari Road, Daryaganj
New Delhi 110 002

Sales Centres:

Allahabad Bengaluru Chandigarh Chennai
Hyderabad Jaipur Kathmandu
Kolkata Mumbai

Typeset in Dante by
Mindways Design
1410 Chiranjiv Tower,
43 Nehru Place
New Delhi 110 019

Printed in India by
Nutech Photolithographers
B-240, Okhla Industrial Area, Phase-I
New Delhi 110 020, India

To Minu

On our tenth anniversary

Contents

Acknowledgements *ix*

Part One

1. The Eclipse 3
2. Three Passengers 15
3. Dwarka to Munirka 25
4. Lost 36
5. A Business Plan 48
6. The Apprentice 57
7. A River of Thoughts 68
8. Crisis 79
9. Fly by Night 88
10. Love and Loss 99

Part Two

11. Homecoming 113
12. The Groom 122
13. Confession 132
14. Aftermath 144

15. Two Generals 153
16. War 160
17. Secret in a Saree 166
18. Key Message 174

Acknowledgements

Every life, they say, is a story.

This story is not about my life but of the people around me. Some have inspired this tale while others have facilitated the production.

I offer my deepest gratitude to the following –

- The Almighty, for endowing me with the necessary faculties to put pen to paper.
- My parents, Mr Ambar Nath Ghatak and Mrs Rina Ghatak, for bringing me into this world and loving me.
- My wife, Meenakshi, and daughter, Devina, for their unending love, support and understanding.
- My late father-in-law, Mr Randhir Singh Rana, who believed I would write a book one day.
- My English teacher, Mrs Lakshmi Seshadri, who taught me that 'modesty is a jewel, rare and precious'. I hope to have lived up to her expectations.
- My publisher, Rupa, for their transparency and efficiency; and editor, Swati Goel, for her patience and diligence.

- Indian Institute of Mass Communication, New Delhi; Presidency College, Kolkata; and the leading advertising agencies of India.
- My friends and colleagues in the PR and advertising world. You guys rock!
- Senior PR professional, Mr Bipul Kiran Singh, for his invaluable lessons on the subject.
- Senior Corporate Communications professional, Mr Amit Chaudhery, for encouraging me to pursue creative writing.

This book would not have happened without you all.

Part One

Chapter 1

The Eclipse

January 2002

Chandni was looking gorgeous. She was wearing an exquisitely embroidered white and peacock green kurti and a matching churidaar. A chiffon dupatta was placed over her head, nicely fixed to the bun that her long hair was tied into. Pieces of gold and silver tinkled from her wrists and ankles as she swayed before the mirror to have a final look. Her face seemed radiant like a full moon in a cloudless sky.

'Come darling, it's time,' winked Garima as she left the room.

Chandni smilingly emerged from the green room into the narrow corridor that led to the stage, only to stop dead in her tracks.

Somashish Mukherjee a.k.a. Som, dressed as the warrior prince Arjuna, was looming like a ghost in the shadows. He was so mesmerised by Chandni that he forgot all else. The love of his life stood before him, adorned in silk and dazzling like a diva. Her large black eyes looked at him with wondrous amazement. Som did not know what to do. As time froze between them, he found a verse emanate from the inner recesses of his molten heart:

O Goddess, your beauty is pristine and unspoilt. I have lost all feeling of sense as I now behold you in your entire magnificence. You are the epitome of love and I long to drown in the nectar of your youth. Your kohl-lined eyes and quivering soft lips beckon me to come to you, hold you, and kiss you. But I can't touch you. Or this magical spell will break.

'Chandni, what the hell!' Garima broke the eternal silence that had seemed to pass in the few seconds that Som and Chandni stood looking at each other. 'And what are you doing here with a raised arrow, smarty?' she scoffed at Som.

As if out of a trance, Som muttered, 'Just wanted to wish her luck.'

He quickly transferred the arrow to his left hand and sheepishly held out the right palm. Chandni let out a shy laugh and took Som's hand into her own. He trembled as he felt the soft warmth of Chandni's skin. But she was gone in the next instant ... Walking away to the call of the Master of Ceremonies.

Som clasped his fingers tightly, determined not to let the warmth escape. *Why didn't he say something to her? Alas, why didn't he pour his heart out?*

'Ladies and gentlemen,' boomed a loud male baritone on the microphone. 'We are happy to begin, with your kind consent, today's charity cultural programme. The final-year students of Presidency College, Kolkata, Arts stream 2002, have put together a rich milieu of dance and drama for your entertainment tonight. We begin with a semi-classical dance rendition of a popular Hindi film song based on the monsoon season. It says and I quote: *Even as the rains beat upon this earth with sound and fury, my beloved is still separated from me. What will I now do, my friend?'*

'Yuck, what language, man,' groaned Arindam Basu under his breath. He was dressed as the mighty Bheema and sat languishing in a corner of the stage. 'Hush,' said Som, 'they're here.'

A beaming Prof. Palash Dasgupta scurried his way off the stage to give way to Garima Dasgupta and Chandni Roy. The two girls moved swiftly in the ensuing darkness to assume their marked positions on stage.

As the lights slowly came back again, strains of mellifluous music filled the auditorium.

Garjat barsat saawan aayo re,
Garjat barsat saawan aayo re,
Laayo na sang mein, hamre bichhde balamwaa,
Sakhi kaa karoon haay, garjat barsat saawan aayo re

'You are listening to All India Radio Vividh Bharati with Lata Mangeshkar and Asha Bhonsle singing to R.D. Burman's music from the film *Pyar Karte Raho,*' mimicked Basu, contorting his face like Prof. Dasgupta.

'Stupid, it's Suman Kalyanpur and Kamal Barot singing to Roshan's music from the film *Barsaat ki Raat,*' protested Som.

'I care two hoots,' retorted Basu.

Som could not be bothered anymore by Basu's diversionary tactics. His eyes were transfixed upon Chandni who now traversed the entire breadth of the stage, sprinting like a doe. Her supple limbs moved with a coordinated precision as her bosom heaved and brows curled in a display of intense longing and passion.

Rimjhim-rimjhim mehaa barse
Tadpe jiyarwaa meen samaan

At this juncture, Chandni twisted and turned her body as if in pain, like a fish pulled out of water. Som stood up spontaneously and the great bow fell from his hand, onto Basu's lap. 'Sit down. She is not calling you.' Basu struck with his elbow.

Som sat down but continued to be in a rapturous state until the thunderous claps of the audience finally awoke him. He rose to his feet as Chandni and Garima made their way back to the green room. Both girls stopped briefly as they crossed him, giggled and then ran away.

Som did not get time to ponder over why they laughed because it was now his turn to be in the limelight. He was soon mouthing a dialogue to Bheema alias Basu:

> *'She has stolen my heart, the sister of Madhav, and I must leave now to rescue her from a miserable marriage to Duryodhana. Please do take care of mother as I leave for Dwarka.'*

AT HIS BEHALA RESIDENCE, Ram Mukherjee sat pensively at the breakfast table, staring at his tea-cup. His wife, Savita, and sons, Somashish and Rahul, sat in abeyance, as if waiting for some announcement. A gentle breeze was blowing into the room from the backyard pond. The house was old and the plaster on the walls had started giving way at random places, revealing a brick here and there.

Ram picked up his worn-out spectacles and spoke slowly. 'Som, you are about to complete your graduation. You soon need to decide on your future course of action. As you know, I have supported your education with whatever little money I had and I also have to keep some for Rahul's GNIIT course.

'You know the job scene in Kolkata. A simple degree is not enough. You must be a doctor or an engineer or an MBA to even stand a chance of earning a decent livelihood. Unfortunately, you missed the CAT exam last year because of jaundice. I think you must appear for the exam this year and try to get into a premier management institute. Even if it is not the IIM, I will try and withdraw money from my PF account to pay for a reputed private institute. I have spoken to your uncle in Delhi and he says there are some good institutes there.'

There was stoic silence for a minute.

'Baba, I want to stay here in Kolkata with all of you. I will try hard for the CAT this year and mark IIM Kolkata as my top preference,' submitted Som. He could not visualise life without his family or Chandni.

Ram Mukherjee looked hard at Som, scrutinising him deeply, assessing the truthfulness and eagerness in his demeanour. 'Well then. Study hard,' he said, rising from his chair and picking up the tea-cup as he left. Savita Mukherjee at once sighed and spoke with relief. 'There is no need to go anywhere. The times are not good. Young Bengali lads are easily misled and spoilt in Dilli's wayward life. Tanushree's son went there five years ago and lives with a Punjabi. Those girls are rough and tough like men, not timid and obedient like us. They control the entire household!'

Rahul smirked and sniffed and covered his face with the newspaper.

'Ma, I'm not marrying a Punjabi girl. And I'm not going anywhere,' said Som, reassuringly placing his hands over Savita's. The mother-son duo then spent the next hour discussing how Som would stay at the IIM campus in Joka and come home to Behala for every vacation.

Savita doted on her elder son, who was her sole pillar of hope and succour. Ram was a distant, reserved husband and wasn't any familiar after twenty-five years of marriage than he was on the wedding night. As Som spoke excitedly, Savita looked with admiring affection at her son's face – large, dark eyes, sharp nose, and a sculpted chin. Had he not been so lanky, Som would have looked like Lord Rama, she thought.

'God save him from the evil eye,' she prayed in her mind.

WHEN IT WAS late afternoon, Som slipped into his jeans and a pair of worn leather sandals and rushed out of home. He hopped into the first tram that came chugging along the Diamond Harbour Road. 'One ticket to Maidaan,' he said to the conductor.

At the Victoria Memorial, Basu, Garima, and Chandni had been waiting for Som at the rear lawns. Basu and Garima were teasing each other and creating a big mess with *phuchka* balls spilling spicy water into their clothes. Chandni sat coyly at a bench, her pink saree gently fluttering in the breeze. She looked at the grand monument, its white marble dome glistening in the afternoon sun.

Just then, Basu's cellphone rang with a loud roar of laughter – his own voice as Bheema. It was Som. '*Kothai*?' he asked.

Minutes later, Som and Chandni stood facing each other in a far corner of the grounds. They both felt a bit embarassed at the sight of numerous young couples engrossed in heavy necking and petting.

'Congratulations! You were fabulous last night,' said Som at last, gathering enough strength to speak to Chandni for the first time.

'Thank you,' said Chandni.

'Why did you want to meet me?' she asked.

Som was stupefied. He had no clear answer. Why did he actually call her? To tell her that he loved her, after three years of absolute silence? After three years of knowing that she was the most sought after girl in the Arts stream? At the fag end of the college term, when each one would go his or her separate way? How could he do so? What would she think of him? He would only make an ass of himself.

And yet, he must tell her, he decided, he must tell her how much he loved her. How he had been secretly watching her all these years. How he remembered every dress she had worn and every dog she owned. How he had spent entire afternoons in the park outside her Tollygunj house, snooping to get just a glimpse of her. How he had even started designing the house they would live in together.

'You … You are very beautiful,' Som mumbled nervously.

Chandni broke into a dry laugh. 'So you called me here just to tell me how beautiful I am?'

'Som,' she said, composing herself, 'you are a good boy and a talented one. All the professors in college have great expectations from you. Every … Everyone has high expectations from you. You should focus on your studies and career now.'

She paused for a moment and continued in a low voice. 'I am getting married next year. Ashok is an M.Tech. from IIT Kanpur and is settled in the US. But you take care and all the best. I'm sure I'll hear from you again.'

The sun had set, painting the sky in hues of brilliant orange and pink. Som's world had just been destroyed and he saw the red debris already up in the sky. 'What a loser I am,' he thought as Chandni gradually walked away from his sight and life.

For several minutes, Som stood motionless. And then, a wave of anger and bitter disappointment engulfed his soul. Furiously enraged and burning all over, he felt an immense hatred towards all IITs and IITians of the world. As he stumbled back to the main road, he looked again at the cavorting couples. He wished to pour kerosene over all of them and set them on fire with Basu's lighter!

He would procure an improvised explosive device from Maoist Shyamalda and destroy this marble edifice which stood in shameless testimony to his first grand failure in life. He would destroy the very essence of this cruel city which could bear to give him so much pain, he thought.

And after he had destroyed everything, he would kill Chandni and then shoot himself in the head.

THE NEXT MORNING, Som was lying inert on his bed.

The golden rays of the sun had permeated into the room and the sparrows chirped away noisily. Savita had kept a glass of milk and some glucose biscuits near the bedside. Som could hear his mother performing puja in the adjacent room, and then blowing a conch shell to herald its completion.

It was the most difficult night that Som had spent so far in his life. In his dream, he repeatedly saw a distressed Chandni being dragged into a luxury car by Ashok Kumar, the M.Tech from IIT. And he could do nothing about it.

'Somu Shona,' Savita called out to him. 'Get up now, my boy. Not having college does not mean you can sleep all day. There are chores to be done and things to be fetched from the market. There is a full lunar eclipse in the evening. Can't venture out then.'

Som did not say anything. He pulled away the sheet and got out of bed. Walking towards his mother, he said, 'Ma, I want to go to Delhi.' Savita was dumbstruck. She turned around and looked at Som's face. 'Are you alright?' she asked, placing the back of her palm against his forehead. 'See, you are running a fever,' she gasped. 'Come, go back to bed. I'll get you a Crocin.'

'Of course he will have fever, walking in a fit of rage from Maidaan to Behala!' thundered Basu as he entered the house. 'I chased him for more than a mile shouting at the top of my voice. But the emperor could not care less!'

Savita and Som looked at the burly guy. 'Aunty, your son has broken his heart in love. He is now the ultimate tragedy king.' Basu spilled the beans. Rahul was playing a football video game in the study. Always looking for an opportunity to get one up on his elder brother, he immediately jumped out to pick on the hot gossip.

Savita listened anxiously to the entire story and then started sobbing uncontrollably. Som was already pale with exhaustion and did little to console her. Rahul shook his head derisively and went back to playing video football. Only Basu tried to infuse some life into the room. 'Let's kidnap the girl. We will take them to Kalighat and get them married there. Then Mr IIT can lick his boots forever.'

'No, no,' said Savita, wiping off her tears. 'We will not commit a wrong for our son's happiness.'

'He is just joking, Ma,' said Som. 'Can't you see the grin on his face?'

'Shona, what we get in life and how much of it we get depend entirely on our fate. I wish I could change your fate. In fact, for the first time, I wish you weren't born to me. You should have been born in a rich family with a palace to live in and rows of servants in attendance,' Savita moaned.

Som was outraged. 'Don't say that please, Ma.' he said. 'Am I to stoop so low as to exchange you for riches?'

He continued in a firm voice. 'It is you who have taught me that a man becomes big by his accomplishments, not by birth alone. That Ashok Kumar, even though he is a pest to me, must have really slogged off his nights to reach wherever he is today. I completely acknowledge that.

'I must stand up on my feet and stand up soon. I had earlier resolved to stay in Kolkata and try to make it to IIM Joka. But I can't take a risk. What if I don't qualify in the CAT? I will have to become a salesman. Kolkata has few other options for me. I will now go to Delhi to become someone, to achieve something. I will put my Hindi classes to good use now. And I will only return once I attain my goal.'

Savita was still in tears but was glad at what her son had said. She excused herself on the pretext of getting the boys something to eat and retreated hastily into the kitchen.

Rahul entered the room again. 'You changed your mind for a girl? Wait until Baba gets wind of this.'

'You will not utter a word of this to anyone, understand? I know your class teacher and I will tell him about the Lara Croft games you play all the time,' threatened Basu.

Caught on the wrong foot, Rahul slithered away again.

Basu got up. 'I must take your leave now, Som. Uncle will be home soon and he doesn't exactly like me around, does he?'

At the door, Basu stopped and turned around. 'Take care,' he said and walked out.

As he was all alone again, Som contemplated his next move. He would have to speak to Shibnath uncle in Delhi to finalise his plans. But he was not keen on an MBA now. He could neither wait for three years nor let his father withdraw his PF money. The household income was barely enough to meet the family's growing needs.

RAM MUKHERJEE WAS a senior accountant with a CA firm in Esplanade and had recently switched jobs to augment his salary. His previous employer of thirty years had fallen on bad days and could not pay annual increments anymore. Unemployment was rampant in the city and the youth took to the streets every now and then to protest. Each time he saw such a procession, Som would remind himself how lucky he was to have a decent education and upbringing. Ashamed of asking his father for pocket money, he gave private home tuitions every alternate day, teaching English, Science, and History to fifth-graders.

As he looked out of the window, Som thought about how he would have to leave everything behind – his parents, friends, students. He would have to start anew and not lose hope. In five years, he would turn around his destiny, earning millions. He would not chase girls. They and their families would chase him instead. But he would marry only the girl who loved him more than herself, willing to completely surrender herself to him.

He took out a graph sheet and began to plot a five-year plan on it. It had an X-axis for income, Y-axis for time, and also a Z-axis indicating relationship status and various stages of progression. 'I should be doubling my income each year, and settle down only after 2007,' he resolved. He was setting himself some very tough financial targets, and also hoped to find true love as he went along. He wanted to show Chandni what she had lost forever. All for one insignificant Ashok Kumar Bhattacharya.

Later that evening, after the family had an unusually quiet dinner, Som lay on his bed gazing at the full moon. He never followed his mother's advice to not look at the eclipsed moon, and tonight as the earth's shadow crept like a blanket over the lunar surface, it seemed to erase all longing for Chandni from Som's mind.

Chapter 2

Three Passengers

Many months later, the Rajdhani Express to New Delhi was waiting at the Howrah station.

A group of passengers had gathered outside the last three-tier air-conditioned coach. A tall, balding man with a large family was banging impatiently on the door, calling for the attendant to open it. Some others egged him on.

After several minutes of incessant banging, the door finally opened. An impish, dark figure emerged from within, looking scornfully at his guests-to-be. A mild altercation ensued, with the irate passengers demanding to know why the door was not opened until about fifteen minutes to departure. The attendant cited some archaic railway rules in his defence, but was losing the war nevertheless.

Basu had come to see off Som. The two friends sat perched on an iron bench on the platform, watching vendors go by and passengers make their way inside the train, even as scores of relatives jostled in and out.

The past twenty-one years of his life in Kolkata flashed before Som's eyes: his ancestral home, the school at Ballygunj, Presidency College, and the umpteen tea-cups at Coffee House on College Steet, arguing about the world's best writer. Som smiled wearily as he remembered all his friends, some bohemian and others normal.

'I will not return unless I become somebody,' said Som, finally standing up. 'Thanks for everything. And please do check on ma at times. Won't you?' Both friends hugged and separated slowly.

Basu took a deep breath, struggling to hold back his tears. 'Let me know your address in Delhi,' he said. 'I will send you an invitation card. Garima and I plan to get married this December after I take over the saree export business.'

'Congratulations!' Som said, happy for his friend. They hugged again.

'Get down fast, the train moves in two minutes,' shouted a hoarse voice from the platform. Som and Basu turned to the door to see the tall baldy get off in a huff. A horde of fathers, mothers, uncles, and aunts followed him, almost falling over each other. By the time Som managed to get a foothold on the stairs, the train was already moving.

Hanging on to dear life, Som heaved himself up the coach. His singular luggage, a VIP suitcase he had bought at a Gariahaat shop, fell on the train floor with a loud thud. Adjusting his spectacles, Som bent down to pick it up but paused midway. A helping hand took the suitcase handle and handed it over to Som.

'Thanks,' said Som as he looked up at the stranger. The smiling gentleman was about forty, wheatish in complexion, and of medium height. He wore silver-framed round glasses and had a bushy salt-and-pepper moustache.

'Most welcome. What is your seat number?' the stranger asked.

'It is fifty-five I think,' said Som, fumbling for his ticket.

'Good, we are together then,' the stranger smiled again.

Som was happy he had got a side berth but unhappy that it was the upper one. He liked to lie down watching the skyline change as the train moved. But now he would be able to sit on the lower berth only when the stranger decided to sleep.

There were six other passengers in that cubicle apart from them. Five of those seemed to be one family – father, mother, two daughters, and a little son. The sixth was a monk, with a shining, shaven head and a saffron shawl wrapped around his well-ordained body.

The woman was looking at the monk with a grateful expression while her husband was yelling on his cell phone in broken Bengali, in a typical dialect of Marwari settlers. The kids were busy feasting on chips and seemed to be most excited about the journey.

The monk had immersed himself in reading an English commentary on the *Gita*.

'Comfortable?' asked the stranger as he spread out his right leg away from Som. Now that they sat facing each other, Som could see he had a deep cut on his chin.

'Yes, sure,' he replied.

'Off to Delhi?'

'Yes.'

Both turned away to the window where the network of rail tracks had given way to clear green fields and mud houses. Small ponds could be seen at places where children were bathing their buffaloes. Groves of banana plantations lined the horizon.

The stranger spoke again, 'The Aravalis around Delhi are dry and rocky, with thorny bushes ruling the landscape. But nothing can match the bounty of the southern Gangetic plains. It comes with the curse of cyclones and floods though.'

Som was getting somewhat interested in the stranger. 'Are you from Delhi or do you travel there frequently?' he asked.

'I live in Delhi. My name is Dr Vibhas Pandey and I am, presently, a professor of History at the Hindu College.'

Som was impressed.

'I am Somashish Mukherjee, Sir,' he said, 'graduate in English Literature from Presidency College, Kolkata.'

'That's great. You make me feel at home, so used I am to blokes of your age.'

Som grinned.

'So, what takes you to Delhi alone?' asked Dr Pandey.

'Search of a career, Sir,' Som said in a low, grim voice.

Dr Pandey raised an eyebrow and then smiled, as if deciphering Som's circumstances. 'MBA? I hope you'll fill the forms for the CAT,' he said.

'I am not sure about an MBA. I don't have two-three years and a lot of money,' explained Som.

'Look, I don't know why you say this but believe me, a good education is a strong foundation to a successful career. If you really are serious about your life, you should not rule out any options. I hate to sermonise, but I suggest you exercise that option unless you want to do an MA and teach English or be a writer,' professed Dr Pandey.

Som thanked him for the advice and promised he would consider it in right earnest. He became interested in knowing more about him, about how he chose his discipline, and about that deep cut on his chin.

'Sir, why did you choose History? As I observe, you could have been a good Geologist as well,' he asked.

The evening had matured into early nightfall, with only dark silhouettes now visible outside the window. Dr Pandey found the question amusing, and prepared to answer as he scratched the back of his head.

'You see, Som,' he began, 'right since childhood, it was important for me to know what I am and why I am so. Where do I belong and what imprint will my community leave in this world. History evaluates everybody. It puts things into a context, a logical serial order, and examines how cultures and civilisations have performed, perished, learnt, and evolved over time. It is man's story. A story that as a human, I ought to bloody well know!'

The train picked up speed as it whistled into the night.

Dr Pandey took a sip from his water bottle and then continued.

'What do we learn from the fall of the Roman Empire? – That conquest alone cannot sustain. Decentralisation and empowerment are necessary. What does the amalgamation of Aryan and Dravidian architecture in South India tell us? It tells us that synergies work wonders, divisions do not. Why did the Mughals wipe out the Rajput rulers of North India? Division of numbers and non-modernisation of weaponry! How could a British trading company defeat us? Actually, they did not. Because the idea of India as a nation never existed, and all that the East India Company did was to annexe and usurp small territories one by one. It is actually a favour that they did us – bringing hundreds of princely states together under Her Majesty's rule.'

'That's true. Some people actually lament the end of British rule,' said Som. 'Look what our politicians have done to us.'

'It is not them alone that we should blame,' cautioned Dr Pandey. 'The founding fathers of our constitution were men of great stature and noble ideas. They carved an excellent platform for the establishment of a truly socialist, democratic state.

'But in every society, there are those who lead and there are others who are led. There cannot exist a power vacuum. When our rulers left, a new ruling class emerged. Like in the feudal past, groups of economically powerful landlords, traders, contractors, and bureaucrats soon wrested control from the common man. We never learnt from history.'

Som thought for a moment.

'You are correct, Sir,' he said. 'Political freedom without education and economic parity means nothing. The subjugated classes got the right to vote but were not in a position to wisely exercise their franchise. They were swayed by money, power, fear of persecution, caste considerations, and religious fervour.'

'Right,' said Dr Pandey. 'What we have today is a subverted democracy. Thanks to the multi-party system, goons and extortionists are also running political outfits. Then there are those who have made it a family business. Sometimes I wonder why people still treat their ministers as kings and queens. They are public servants, dammit!'

'But Sir, does history have all the answers we seek?' asked Som.

'Not all. But the past is always a guide. And it holds out hope too. Scientists today are developing lines of treatment for AIDS in the hope that they will succeed one day, just as they successfully surmounted killers like cancer, malaria, and cholera.'

'Not cancer. It still kills,' said a third voice.

Dr Pandey and Som turned in surprise towards the monk seated on the edge of seat number forty-eight, a couple of feet away from them.

'Well, not all cancers kill,' argued Dr Pandey.

'Yes, but most cancers still do,' said the monk calmly.

Suddenly, there was tension in the air. Dr Pandey, who was waxing eloquent with all his intelligent talk, was abruptly interrupted by a monk who wanted to prove a point. The householder's wife was now gaping at them as if a bullfight was to ensue. The kids and their father stopped their game of ludo to check if all was fine.

Som decided to defuse the tension a bit.

'Swamiji, you seem to have a personal perspective on this,' he said to the monk.

The monk in saffron robes had beautiful, lotus-like eyes and sharp features. The expression in them was peaceful and contemplative. He looked at Som and addressed him in a deep, calm voice.

'Somashish, that's your name, right?' he continued. 'The point is not about whether cancer is curable or not. The question is – can we find a cure for each and every disease that nature throws at us? Can we evade the inevitability that is born with us when we come into this world? Can we avoid disaster, wear and tear, accident, and death? No, we cannot. Mere knowledge of the entire past or of the ensuing future cannot make us any wiser. History repeats itself and the vicious cycle continues.'

Dr Pandey could not hold it within himself any longer. 'If everything is so futile, Swamiji, what is the use of existence? Why do people even live in hope and pray?'

Som was getting worried now. He felt strangely drawn towards both and felt sorry that the discussion was heading towards an imminent showdown.

'Professor,' the monk said, 'history may guide us and teach us, but no knowledge or learning is adequate enough to deliver us from our mortal limitations. There is a grand scheme of things, and we are but pawns in the great game.'

'You mean destiny is everything, action is nothing, Swamiji?' asked a bewildered Som.

'No, but the wisdom to do the right action is not commonly available in the market. It is only when man admits his physical and mental limitations and surrenders to the Supreme that he will realise his true self and potential. Infinite possibilities lie within the soul that refuse to be bound by ego-consciousness and ultimately merges into the Master,' clarified the monk.

'*Aham Amritasya Putraha,* say the sages – I am the son of the immortal!' he exclaimed. 'Some of them also said *Tat Tvam Asi* – Thou Art That, and devotees of the Lord always sit at His feet.'

'Excuse me, Som,' said Dr Pandey, and got up from his seat.

'Professor Pandey is angry, Som,' said the monk as his eyes followed the man out of the compartment. 'Sorry, I could not prevent myself from intruding in your discussion. I have been through these thoughts and queries so many times in my youth that I cannot help but offer what I have learnt.'

'No, that's fine, I guess,' mumbled Som as he saw the family sitting frozen together, looking startled by the debate and the utterance of Sanskrit phrases.

'Before I became Swami Swarup Damodar Das, I was a surgeon with the best hospital in the US – Johns Hopkins. And yet, with all my skill and learning, I could not save my wife from succumbing to breast cancer. For many years thereafter, I dwelt upon the fundamental issues of life until I found eternal light in Sri Krishna.

'Now that Bhagwaan shows me through his eyes and leads me by his stick, I have no worries. So stupid I was, despairing over her death. The soul never dies. It goes on, dancing to my Master's flute.'

The family had now folded palms in obeisance to the monk.

'My station is here, Som. I need to go,' said the monk. 'But you should ask professor about the cut in his chin. Lucky escape he had. Gopala saved him that day.

'And remember not to benchmark yourself to others' lives. There is nothing we have to achieve except to understand our true selves.'

As the monk got up, everybody else got up too. The family touched his feet one by one. He blessed each of them, and to the householder he said, 'Please don't put my ma through another suffering. Sons and daughters are all the same.'

And then he was gone, with just a small sack in hand.

Shortly afterwards, Dr Pandey emerged with two bottles of cola. 'I went to the pantry. Needed to cool off,' he laughed. 'Swamiji has vanished I see,' he said mockingly.

'Yes, he got off at Dhanbad,' replied Som.

After the third sip, when Dr Pandey seemed completely relaxed and the family was not looking their way, Som put forth the million dollar question.

'If you don't mind, Sir,' he said, 'what's that deep cut on your chin?'

'Oh yes, I almost died that day,' smiled Dr Pandey.

'Some dacoits broke into our house in Bihar and everybody tried to hide. Those who could not, were brutally slaughtered. I found the prayer room open and dashed inside. As I raced, I slipped on offerings of peeled bananas and fell at the foot of a Krishna idol.

'My chin suffered a deep cut and I lay there unconscious for over an hour. I survived only because I lay unseen in a corner. Had I been awake, I would not have had the guts to lie still on the floor for so much time.'

Som almost choked in amazement. 'So the Swami was right,' he said.

'What do you mean?' asked a puzzled Dr Pandey.

The following conversation was lost in the din of dinner.

Chapter 3

Dwarka to Munirka

At about ten in the morning, the train chugged into the New Delhi railway station.

Dr Pandey and Som took leave of each other and parted ways. As directed by his uncle, Shibnath Mukherjee, Som exited the platform from the Paharganj side and made his way out of the station complex.

In the utter chaos outside, a green bus was preparing to leave for Dwarka. Without wasting a second, Som hurled himself up the bus. Choosing a seat at the back, he placed his suitcase under it. Comfortably seated, he looked outside at the capital of India, as it presented itself from the window.

Initially, the scene at Paharganj was not unlike any street in Kolkata, with utter chaos reigning at the traffic signal and taxis, autos, and bullock carts jostling for space. But within minutes, as the bus moved into Connaught Place and onward into Lutyen's planned zone, Som was surprised to observe the stark differences.

Besides the vast, open, planned spaces and the apparent lack of filth, what struck Som was the way people dressed and walked about. In a sharp contrast to the casual and careless kurta-jhola or shirt-hung-over-pants style of his native city, the youth in Delhi seemed dressed for an occasion and moved around with a positive, overtly aggressive body language. The men here seemed taller and broader, and the younger women did not wear sarees at all. In fact, some ladies were quite modestly covered and could easily earn public ire back in Kolkata.

Compared to the legacy wood-and-aluminum buses back home, Delhi had green CNG buses that looked monstrous but no way rickety. The taxis too seemed to be in better shape and so did the drivers. Brightly lit shops were neatly arranged, like in Park Street in Kolkata. There was greenery all around and no sight of slums yet. Som was impressed.

He knew at once that he had come to a city that lives well, presents well, and is at least decades ahead of the former capital of India. 'Thank you, Communists,' Som muttered bitterly to himself. Bengal had missed the bus to development, he knew.

As he slightly leaned back his head on the seat, he was immersed in the thoughts of how he would carve his own place and career in this alien city, and how he would challenge life itself.

THAT EVENING, THERE was a party at the second-floor flat of Aurobindo Apartments at Sector 14, Dwarka. The host, Shibnath Mukherjee, was busy introducing his nephew to guests and neighbours. There were his colleagues from the Ministry of Defence – Mr Sharma, Mr Katyal, Mrs Iyer, and friends from the local Kali temple association – Chanchal Ghosh and Swapan Banerjee. Chanchal's daughter Aparna was also around, helping the hostess with snacks. She was quite tall for a Bengali girl, and had a wheatish complexion and thin, black hair.

Shibnath's retirement was a week away and he thought of this gathering as a means to both welcome Som to Delhi and bid his friends adieu. In about a fortnight, he and his wife Mukta would fly away to the US to their son, Manik, who worked in a software start-up there.

The discussion in the drawing room was presently focussed on what line of education or career Som should pursue. And where he should live after the Mukherjees were gone to the US.

Mr Sharma bent down to dip his pakora in tomato sauce and then, looking at Som, he said, 'I think you should appear for the Bank Probationary Officers exam.'

'No, no,' Mr Katyal cut him short. 'If he is talented, he must take the CAT this year. An MBA will take only two years if he makes it, and if his father is ready to fund it, what is the problem? He will earn it back within months!'

'But an MBA is not enough in itself. Suppose he majors in marketing, what sector does he choose at the campus placement? FMCG and manufacturing are not hot these days. Insurance and technology are. But in those companies, they desire knowledge of finance or IT,' opined Mrs Iyer. 'My son struggled for two years at this chyavanprash company before he got into Wipro,' she added for good measure.

'Having been with the Government for so long, I don't know of any options other than MBBS, engineering, or MBA. Manik did his software engineering, and see how well he is doing now!' said Shibnath finally.

'What do you want to do, young man?' asked Chanchal Ghosh, finishing off the fish cutlet. Aparna was now seated besides him, gently smiling at Som.

'I honestly do not know,' quipped Som, feeling a bit pressurised. 'What do you suggest?' he turned to Aparna in hope.

Even though she was a little older to Som, Aparna was mindful of not openly contesting the views of the elders. She thought for a second and then spoke slowly, 'What everyone is saying is true. If you consider conventional choices, then MBA is an obvious option. But there are some unconventional and upcoming career options too. And you're lucky that Delhi has quite a few institutes that offer such choices.'

'What are you talking about, Apu?' asked Chanchal.

All eyes in the room turned towards Aparna, as if only she could salvage Som's life.

'Well,' began Aparna. 'You all know that I am pursuing research in biotechnology from the National Institute of Immunology. A few yards from my institute is the Indian Institute of Mass Communication. I regularly see many students going there and once, one of them told me she was training to become an advertising copywriter. Som is an English literature graduate and, from what I heard, the money seems good.'

Nobody had a comment to offer. They did not have the faintest idea of what a copywriter did, and could not be bothered anymore. The sun had set and the guests had to leave.

Only Swapan stayed back. 'I know someone living in Munirka. He needs a room partner. If you study near where Aparna goes, you should rather stay at Munirka. Let me know,' he said to Som. And then, he too departed.

Som felt joyous. He was very happy with Aparna's advice. 'Mass Communication it shall be then,' he thought. '*Jethu*, do you have Internet?' he asked Shibnath.

That night, Shibnath spoke to Ram Mukherjee on phone, assuring all would be well with Som. His wife was back in the kitchen, preparing *shorshe-ilish* and gushing over how much Manik loved it.

Som was lost in the web world, searching every corner of the Internet for information on Mass Communication. Finally, after hours of research, it was a toss-up among three institutes – IIMC, Amity Business School, and Jamia Milia Islamia's Media Studies Centre. But Som was in a hurry. He could not wait to complete a two-year course. It had to be IIMC's one-year PG Diploma in Advertising and PR.

Set up with the help of specialists from UNESCO and the Ford Foundation, the IIMC was opened in 1965 by Mrs Indira Gandhi, the late prime minister, Som read. 'It has to have class and a good curriculum,' he mused, browsing further through its home page. Soon afterwards, he was a bit put off by some freak spelling and grammar mistakes on the site. 'What a pity,' he thought. 'Let me get there and I'll point these out.'

He called up Aparna and set an agenda for the very next morning.

APARNA WAS DRIVING the scooty at a brisk speed. Som sat quietly behind her, leaning backwards to hold the spare tyre, careful not to fall on her back at every speed-breaker. A couple of times he could not help it though. He said sorry whenever he brushed against her and after the third time, Aparna said, 'Don't bother, silly.'

The scooty made its way from Dwarka to the Palam village flyover. The June sun was sizzling.

'So, what sort of hurry are you exactly in, Som?' Aparna teased. 'Has your girlfriend's father given you an ultimatum or something? You are just twenty-one!'

'No, it's not that. I don't have a girlfriend, you see. The reason I didn't want to wait for the next year and then spend two more years studying is that I know the condition at my home, and I know how Baba struggles to make both ends meet. Moreover, if I have to pay a hefty fee to a private institute, it does not make any sense. Not to me. Not if there are other roads to success,' Som explained.

'Oh, I see. You're the perfect Bong elder son types,' said Aparna. 'But wait for a year and I'll ask you about your girlfriend again. I shall see how you respond then.'

Both of them laughed and Som was again lost in thoughts. He could see the vehicles on the road were newer and brighter than Kolkata, and the drivers were better-dressed. Palam village appeared to be in a little mess though, quite like his neighbourhood in Kolkata. They soon crossed the airport and were now heading to the Outer Ring Road.

At the first Vasant Vihar red light, a black car halted beside them on the left with a loud screech. Both turned to look. At first, they could see nothing but their own reflections on the tinted, dark glass window. Then slowly, the window rolled down three inches. A loud blare of music came from inside. '... *Kabhi mere saath koi raat guzaar, tujhe subaha tak main karoon pyaar, oh oh oh* ...' sang a nasal male voice.

Som felt embarrassed. The lyrics were being thrown at Aparna. 'How disgusting,' he thought. A few bikers on their right smiled knowingly, enjoying Aparna's predicament.

'Bastard!' yelled Aparna.

Som got a bit nervous. He had not been in such a situation before in life. Angered by Aparna's abuse, the driver rolled down the window.

'What did you say, bitch? Let me cool you down,' the driver shouted as he held out his arm to nab Aparna. Som could see a dark, unshaven face with long, back-brushed hair. A diamond twinkled in the man's right ear.

Aparna's reaction was immediate. She moved away her hand and quickly drove off to the right, towards Vasant Vihar C-Block market. Som almost fell off backwards, but recovered somehow from the shock. Immediately, a traffic constable came whistling after them.

Aparna applied the brakes and turned around to see where the car was. He had initially followed them but on seeing the cop, the driver had taken a U-turn and fled away.

Som noted the number plate. It ended with the numerals 5100 and had 'Punjab Police' written on top. The rear windshield had the words 'Vicky te Soni di Gaddi' inscribed in bold white letters.

'What are you upto? You could have caused a serious accident, jumping the red light like this!' scolded the constable.

'Didn't you see he was harassing me?'

The following exchange did not make sense. The constable yelled at Som, '*Tanne koi sharm naa say*? Aren't you ashamed of riding backseat? You should learn to protect your girlfriend.'

It felt worse than the slap he had got in class two from the music teacher.

Aparna stopped talking and decided to drive off.

After ten minutes or so, she stopped the scooty just outside the entrance to the IIMC. 'Life is meant to be tough, Som. It's not about the city. Go in and give me a call once you are done,' she said.

Som was shaken and wondered if he had committed the biggest mistake of his life by coming to Delhi. But Aparna was unfazed and strong. Som respected her for that and got off in silence.

'Thank you,' he said as she managed a smile and whizzed off.

Gathering his wits and reminding himself of his core purpose in life, Som slowly walked towards the idol of Goddess Saraswati encased in glass on the right side of the iron gate.

There, he folded his palms together and recited a Sanskrit hymn in praise of the Goddess.

'Yaa Kundendu tushaara haaradhavalaa, Yaa shubhravastraavritha ...

May Goddess Saraswati,
Who is fair like the jasmine-coloured moon,
Whose pure white garland is like frosty dew drops,
Who is adorned in a radiant white attire,
On whose beautiful arms rests the veena,
And whose throne is a white lotus,
Who is surrounded and respected by the Gods, protect me.
May you fully remove my lethargy, sluggishness, and ignorance.'

Som made a solemn promise to himself. He would fight it out until he accomplished something and became someone. He would not go back, whatever the difficulties, whatever the tribulations.

The room of the Officer-on-Special-Duty was empty when Som entered with his papers. He waited for five long minutes, gazing at the walls, and then decided to search elsewhere. On his way out, he almost bumped into a burly, middle-aged man at the door.

'PG Diploma for Advertising and Public Relations?' asked the professor. 'I don't know why you people wait until the last day.'

ON REACHING MUNIRKA, Aparna and Som waited at the sweet shop near the main road. Swapan had said that Kenneth Rodrigues would be there shortly. Feeling farnished, the two decided to feast on hot samosas and jalebis. A light drizzle began outside. Soon, bikers and scooterists were scrambling for cover from the unpredicted rain. With nowhere else to go, some of them entered the sweet shop, shaking water off their bodies.

'Are you Aparna?' asked a male voice. Som and Aparna looked over their shoulders to find a long, dark face smiling at them from behind a pair of thin-rimmed spectacles. The man had a canopy of curly brown hair on his head.

'Hi, I'm Kenny,' the guy said. 'Mr Banerjee told me you're dressed in a blue kurta, so I figured out. Actually, I taught guitar to his daughter last year,' he continued to smile, slightly flashing his pearl-white teeth.

'Hello. Yes I am Aparna and this is Som,' she said, holding out her hand to Kenny.

Minutes later, the three were sipping hot tea at Kenny's rooftop *barsati* in a four-storey house.

''This place looks good and cosy,' Som said.

'Of course, it is, Som. It gets enough sun, air, and the rain, and there's a spectacular view of the neighbouring terraces and the main road. You can sing, dance, and make merry all day without anybody bothering you,' Kenny said.

'But there's only one hazard,' he warned. 'You will have me for company and I will create a lot of noise using this thing,' he said, holding up his acoustic guitar.

'Why, that's perfectly fine with me,' Som said excitedly. 'I might even want to learn from you,' he added.

'Five thousand rupees a month for that,' quipped Kenny.

'And how much is the rent?' asked Aparna.

'Oh, that's two thousand a month. Fifty per cent of the total.'

'That's a deal then. I move in this Sunday,' beamed Som.

Kenny was happy. 'Welcome in! I have my classes at the YMCA on Sunday mornings, so I'll leave the keys with the landlady on the ground floor,' he said.

Taking a sip from his steel glass, Kenny remembered something. 'Actually, do meet the lady on your way back. She has some interesting residency rules here, including one that forbids entry of unrelated women after dark.'

Aparna frowned. *Why is the world so hung up about the male-female relationship? Are people animals that they cannot be simply friends? Why does a girl have to be kept outside after dark? Are they all nymphomaniacs or what?* She thought.

Even before she could decide whether to get involved in meeting the landlady, there was a loud knock on the door.

Kenny unbolted the door to find a massive woman standing on the terrace. He smiled. 'Come aunty, we were just coming to you.'

The lady was not amused in the least. '*Yo chori kaun say aur yeh baalak kaun say*?' she demanded. 'Why have you bolted the door? What were you three doing in here?'

Aparna turned her face away in disgust.

'Manju aunty,' Kenny pleaded. 'Please understand. Som, here, is my new room-partner. And Aparna is a family friend. Rain water was coming into the room and I had to bolt the door. Don't you trust me even after three years? Have I ever done any hanky-panky here?'

Aparna felt the explanation insulting. 'I'll wait for you at the sweet shop, Som,' she said as she got up and left.

Manju's eyes followed Aparna until she disappeared down the winding staircase.

Then she turned towards Som, and said, 'Be careful. I will watch over you. As long as you want to study, you can live here. The day I catch you doing hero-giri, you'll be thrown out. *Samajh aaya tanne*?'

Som nodded his head in acceptance.

That night, he bought a local SIM card and called home. Savita was overwhelmed with emotion and could barely speak. 'Ma, why do you cry?' he consoled. 'Everything is going well here. I have applied at IIMC and if I clear the test, I will get admission. The course will be done by March. I have also found a nice, cheap place to stay in. Jethu's friend knows my room-mate well. What more can I ask for? By next Durga Puja, I will return to you – successful!'

Ram Mukherjee too spoke to his son.

'I am sending some money to your uncle. He will get your savings account opened before he leaves for the US. Take care.' This was all he managed.

'Send me some nice video games next month. There is a Ninja turtle game you will find at a place called Palika Bazaar,' ordered Rahul.

Som smiled and looked up at the sky. It was again a full moon night. But there was no eclipse this time.

Chapter 4

Lost

Time, they say, waits for none.

Somashish Mukherjee sat waiting at the Ogilvy & Mather office.

Almost a year had passed since he had arrived in the city. In these past four seasons, Som had seen Delhi in all its myriad hues and multiple shades. Every experience seemed new. Every moment was a small revelation.

He had enjoyed the long, wet drizzles of the monsoon, counting the many bright orange blooms on the Gulmohars outside his class. He had loved getting drenched under a vast grey sky, standing all alone in nothing but a brief. And he had absolutely loved the endless cups of steaming hot coffee at the IIMC canteen.

Som remembered how, as autumn came, Kenny got very busy. He found a steady flow of musical assignments coming his way. He would get invited to either play solo at a party or join a Rock group at some concert. And when Som was not pouring over his books, he would jam with Kenny on a Jamaiican drum. Kenny would sing *'Down the way, where the nights are gay …'* It was real bliss.

Aparna was a regular visitor to their rooftop residence. Of course, she always came by the day and wore only salwaar kurtas. But whenever she came, she got along a host of goodies and small utilities. The boys loved it. The three were one happy family until the end of autumn.

A day after Diwali, while Som had gone to refill the cooking gas cylinder, Manju aunty apprehended Aparna and Kenny in an apparently compromising position. Kenny had protested, explaining he was only trying to blow off a speck of dust from Aparna's eye. Aunty did not relent. She called in Surajmal, the local strongman, and threw Kenny's belongings down the terrace.

That winter was severely harsh on Som. He spent the next three months in solitary confinement, without a room partner. He had not felt so cold ever, used as he was to the moderate winters back home. When the mercury dipped to four degrees around Christmas, he suffered a bout of mild pneumonia. Taking pity on him, Manju aunty called Kenny and Aparna. They rushed in hand-in-hand, without the slightest guilt or remorse.

Kenny had landed a permanent job at the YMCA and now stayed in an apartment in Patparganj in East Delhi. They immediately shifted Som out of Munirka to Kenny's new home. That was the last Som saw of Munirka's dingy bylanes, leaning buildings, budget eateries, and quaint video shops.

He really missed the place afterwards.

Ram Mukherjee wanted to visit his son in Delhi but Som forbade him from doing so. Savita almost died when she heard of Som's illness. For the next eleven days, she would wake every day at 4.30 a.m. to offer special prayers at the local Shiva temple. Basu and Garima, now on their honeymoon, called Som from Kathmandu. And Shibnath Mukherjee called from Phoenix.

It had taken over a month for Som to fully recover from his illness. By February, he was fit as a fiddle. On Basant Panchami, he performed a recitation of Tagore's poem, '*Where the mind is without fear and the head is held high ...*', to a thunderous applause at the MANCH auditorium at IIMC. His Hindi was now better than ever before, and he also contributed an acclaimed piece to the college's bi-annual journal, *Sanchaar Maadhyam*. The essay was titled '*Hindi Sahitya Mein Naaree Ka Charitra*'.

Out of the ten papers in his syllabus comprising communications, PR, and advertising, Som had problems with only one subject. He found the Advertising Creativity and Campaign Planning classes very subjective. For example, he could not understand why the purists advocated against the use of reverse printing while most catchy ads in papers had white text against a black background.

Spring did not last long. The exams were over and summer was at hand. The Dahlias in the IIMC garden had disappeared, and cuckoos could be heard cooing in the Sanjay Van across the Aruna Asaf Ali road.

On the day of Holi, Chanchal Ghosh announced the engagement of Aparna and Kenny with much fanfare. 'Apu is all I have. How can I see her unhappy?' Chanchal said to the gathering, wiping off his moist eyes.

The couple was moved at his magnanimity and the liberal bent of mind. Aparna did not leave her father's side that entire afternoon. Kenny sat with Som in a corner, chatting about his future plans. He revealed he would join a media production house in Mumbai and Aparna would take up a job with a biotech firm there. 'By the way, I was really trying to remove dust from Aparna's eyes that day. The fact that I loved her occurred only after I was thrown out and did not see her for a month,' Kenny confided.

Som smiled, and suddenly realised he had to quickly find a job and a new house. For days, he searched on the net and read all job supplements, but found nothing suitable. He tried cold calling but that too didn't work. Finally, he created a portfolio of articles, poems, ideas, and sketches and dispatched copies to all the big advertising agencies in Delhi.

AND NOW HERE he was, sitting at the reception of O&M, along with half a dozen other applicants.

'Somashish Mukherjee,' called the receptionist. 'First turn right, please,' she said. .

Som straightened out his cuffs and collar and proceeded to enter the glass meeting room. Pretty office, he thought. And pretty good people too.

Inside, a bearded man, probably in mid-thirties, was swivelling in the chair.

'Come in, son,' the man said.

They shook hands. 'Nikhil Jaitley,' the interviewer said.

'Just be easy, I won't eat you up. This is not a zoo or amphitheatre. And you could have wandered in here in a T-shirt. How do I care? It's immaterial to me. The question is whether you are original and thoughtful as a copywriter. There's no good copy or bad copy. I mean, if the syntax is right, any copy is good enough. What really matters is when I read it, do I feel a pulse? Does your sentiment excite me, does it engage me? Do your words cry out for attention? It should leave people engaged; they should either hate it or love it. There's nothing called middle earth. This is no *Lord of the Rings* contest. We judge you by the spark and see if you can ignite us. Come, show me,' Nikhil said.

Som sat stunned at the discourse. But he was happy he'd finally got an opportunity to speak. 'Here, Sir, is my portfolio of dummy ads. Print, jingles, storyboard...'

'No *Sir* business here, OK?' Nikhil cut him short.

'Kids do this as homework in school. I don't want to see these.' He flung the folder back to Som.

He continued, 'We have seen enough of these simulated brainwork. It is so artificial. If you are serious about a career in advertising, lad, forget all your past conditioning. Just let go of yourself. Who wants to read the crap that we see in magazines everyday? Bring me something fresh, something outrageous, radical, totally neurotic.'

'But ... but,' Som tried to interject.

'Look, we are busy people and charge for our time. If I take you as my junior copy guy, I want to see what value you will add,' Nikhil said.

'I give you a situation here. Think of it carefully. You are the creative director of this company. The client wants to design a New Year calendar and gives you a week to do it. The premise is that this calendar should perk up the sale of its oral contraceptive. Now tell me what you would do.'

Som thought hard for a while. Lifting his chin up, he said, 'I think I will get a young couple to pose for photographs in the most romantic of places – Kashmir, Ooty, Udaipur, and the theme would harp on togetherness and the peace of mind that comes with family planning.'

'Such a conditioned answer,' said Nikhil. 'You know what I would do? I'll shoot the same couple in the same places, but with the man in each photo bound in a giant condom. The message is – switch to pills, shed the cover, get really up, close, and personal. Now that's what I call advertising!'

Som felt entirely good-for-nothing.

As he walked back to the reception dejectedly, the next candidate hopped by him. She was wearing a tight, bright-red T-shirt, painted with the words 'B(P)UN INTENDED!'

'Wrong spelling but quite radical,' Som thought.

The Mudra Communications office at Safdarjung Enclave was located in a nice, big bungalow. The peon was exceptionally polite and got a glass of chilled water for Som. The air-conditioning was super-effective in keeping out the sultry Delhi heat. People smiled as they moved about. The atmosphere was calm and rejuvenating.

'Are you Somashish?' asked a short gentleman in a blue half-sleeve shirt. He looked only a few years older than Som, and was fair and stocky. 'Come, we'll find a room for ourselves.'

'I am Manish Gupta,' the man said, sitting on a couch. There was something dispassionate and calm about him.

'Nice to meet you,' said Som.

They talked about IIMC, where Manish too was once a student. 'I hope professor Jaiswal is doing well. Do greet him when you meet him next,' said Manish.

'Sure, I will,' replied Som. He was at ease and feeling at home.

'So, tell me about yourself.'

Som started from his childhood days, teenage years, and college in Kolkata, enumerating all the things he was fond of doing and all the competitions he had won.

'So, what do you like doing most?'

'I like travelling, singing, reading, writing, sketching ... all of it,' said Som.

'Has somebody ever hurt you badly?'

Som thought of Chandni for a second, but said, 'Not really.'

'What would you do if you were in office working on a very important project and someone told you your mother is sick at home?'

'Well, I would call my brother and other relatives for help, and tell them I'll finish work and join them soon,' said Som.

Manish was not pleased. 'Had I been in your place, I would have left everything and rushed to my mother,' he said.

Can any of my answers today be right at all? Som thought.

'Look Somashish. To tell you the truth, it is my last day here today. I'm off to the Gulf tomorrow. But I'll mark my evaluation as I go. I don't know who will follow up on the case, but all the best nevertheless!'

He smiled at Som and left the room after shaking hands.

Som was in a tizzy. He could not understand why Manish had interviewed him when he was no longer with the company, and also how could he evaluate someone on the basis of three personal questions.

Disappointed, he set out into the blazing sun again. He had eaten nothing since morning, moving from one ad agency to the other.

RAJAT AHLUWALIA STOOD at six feet three inches. As the senior copywriter of the country's most awarded creative agency, he surely was head and shoulders above others. He also seemed to be the busiest advertising professional Som had met so far.

Crouching in a corner of the somewhat congested McCann Erickson office in Zamrudpur, Som was keenly following every conversation Rajat was having on the phone.

'Try some French word for the soap ... Something that is spoken from the roof of the mouth, not the throat. That will lend an exotic, upmarket feel to the brand,' Rajat counselled someone on his mobile.

'Sorry Sir,' he finally said to Som. 'How may I help you today?'

'I had actually wanted to apply for the position of a junior copywriter here and I was referred to you,' said Som.

'I see,' said Rajat. 'But I'm sorry we have no vacancies currently. I'd be bluffing if I said otherwise. The fact is, however good you may be, we just don't have enough place to sit here.'

Som was crestfallen.

Rajat looked at Som's pale face and suddenly changed his mind. 'But alright, let me check you first. Let me put you through our standard copy test and see how you score, OK?'

Som's face lit up again. At least he would know where he stood.

The copy test was less intimidating than he had expected. He had to do five tasks.

Task 1– *Write a campaign for a brand of organic foodgrains that are 30 per cent more expensive than the market.*

Task 2– *Create an election slogan for a regional political party representing salt workers of Kutch.*

Task 3– *Write a TV ad storyboard for a new washing powder that keeps hands soft.*

Task 4– *Write an eight-line radio jingle for pure cotton vests and briefs.*

Task 5– *Create a magazine ad for Golden Sands Beach Resort, Karwar*

After ninety minutes, Som ran down to the ground floor where Rajat was taking a smoke break.

'Hmm, let's see,' Rajat remarked.

After a few minutes, he threw the cigarette stub on the ground and pressed it with his right toe. 'You are good, Som,' he said. 'But, as I told you, we have no vacancy for trainees. However, there are some agencies that are looking for people like you, and I can refer you to them. Does that work for you?'

Tears of gratitude welled up in Som's eyes. He nodded.

Pink Dot Advertising was tucked in the basement of a large mansion in Alaknanda. It was very difficult to find it unless one spotted a fleet of stairs going down from behind a bottle palm tree.

Two brothers, Swaraj and Viraj Bhandari, owned the agency.

While Swaraj would get the clients and brief the team on what was required, Viraj was entrusted with administrative responsibilities.

Som showed Rajat's 'letter of recommendation' to Swaraj. 'Good,' he said. 'Join today, now.'

Som's happiness knew no bounds. In the excitement and gratitude, he forgot to even ask the salary amount. Soon, he was sitting at his own desk – The Copy Desk – and going through the tasks at hand.

An assistant came with tea and some joining papers, including PF nomination forms. Som could not believe he had landed his first job as a copy head with a salary of twenty thousand rupees per month.

Remembering God and his parents, he picked up the pen to write.

NEXT DAY, SWARAJ was in a gruffy mood. Clients had been sending work back to the agency, not liking either the visuals or the copy. Long-term partners like Handicrafts Promotion Council, RJ Microelectronics, and Aqua Fittings had threatened to move their businesses elsewhere if things did not improve.

Som was summoned to Swaraj's cabin.

'Here, this is the basic text for the two ads you will do today. The RJ appointments ad will be a half-page one in the job supplement, and HPC will be for the inside cover of *Times Today*. Chaitanya will do the visuals. A couple of past ads are placed on your table. Go, take a look,' Swaraj said.

Som was a bit surprised. Is this the only briefing he would get? What about brand positioning and tone of communication? How would the visuals sync with the copy? Could he break away from the past approach and suggest a fresh one?

Som thought long and hard, and decided he would maintain continuity and only polish up the text. After half-a-day's hard work, the ads were ready – two options for each one.

Swaraj examined all four sheets repeatedly. He was not satisfied. 'There's no spark in them. Put in some life,' he said.

Som went back to his desk and started all over again.

Viraj stood guard at the entrance to the basement, watching each of the dozen employees closely.

Several hours and versions later, Som was still at it. Swaraj had rejected all options on the ground that they were not exciting enough. No further explanation was forthcoming.

Tired, exhausted, and demoralised, Som crept out of the basement for dinner. As he bit into an egg-roll at the nearby food van, he was filled with a compelling desire to run, to quit, to escape the depressing dungeon called Pink Dot Advertising.

And so, he did not return.

Som walked as fast as he could towards C R Park. He did not turn back for the fear that Viraj could be following him. When he had walked as far as Savitri cinema, he stopped to rest. From there, he hopped onto a minibus to Nehru Place. Finally, as he boarded a DTC bus to East Delhi, Som felt like a convict who has escaped his sentence in prison.

In the morning, he realised what he had done. He had quit the first job in his life on the very second day. A job that had taken a year of education and training to find. A job that was to be the starting point to a great career. He blew it completely. What a loser he was indeed!

What would he do now? Where would he go? How would he face his parents and the world?

He went for his wallet and took out a crumpled sheet of paper. It was his five-year plan. It was 2003 and he had set a salary target of five lakh for himself by the end of the year. The beginning was great. It was 2.4 lakh – but he had completely ruined it.

Som thought about that fateful day when he had decided to come to Delhi.

With a year gone and thousands of rupees spent by his father on his study and living, Som had achieved nothing. He could not see a road ahead. It was as if he had failed and Chandni had won.

After all, she was only practical in marrying a highly educated, well-settled boy. What chance did a loser like Som have?

Chapter 5

A Business Plan

With nothing else to do, Som began checking his mails on Kenny's computer.

That done, he opened every job site that he knew of, and ran a search for all advertising and marketing positions. Unfortunately, there were no jobs for freshers.

Frustrated and now feeling a bit on the edge, Som started calling his classmates at IIMC.

The class topper, S. Muthukumaran, had landed a correspondent's job with a leading English newspaper in Delhi. Most other good students had found employment with either an ad agency or a media house. One of them had joined an international NGO.

'I am the only loser around,' Som muttered.

He weighed his options. He would have to call his mother and tell her everything. He had hit a roadblock and didn't know how or when he would be on track again.

Som looked at his cellphone lying on the bed. It was almost out of charge, and had a meagre ten rupee balance. 'Spent force,

I don't have the money to recharge. Now, let's finally do it. Dial ma.'

As soon as he proceeded to press a button, the phone sprang to life. It was Bhaskaran, an IIMC batchmate, who had dropped out in the second month.

'What's up, Som?' asked Bhaskaran in a jovial voice.

'Was just trying to hang myself,' replied Som.

'What?'

Som told him his story in short: the interviews at the ad agencies, his first job, and then the disappointment. Before Bhaskaran could suggest a solution, the phone went dead.

'Ha, nice luck!' cried Som.

The doorbell rang at half past two. Som was jolted out of his slumber. He had gone to sleep in the bizarre hope that he would find some direction in a dream. Often, it had happened that he had found new ideas and inspirations in his dreams. So, he had dozed off on a hungry stomach.

But the dream he had that afternoon was more of a nightmare. He saw he was still in high school and was late for the math paper. By the time he reached the exam centre, he remembered nothing from the syllabus.

A sweaty Som opened the doorknob. Outside, stood a tall, dark boy in a business suit and pony tail.

'Hey, you came here all the way thinking I'd die?' squealed Som in amazement.

'Boss, there's an urgent meeting I want you to attend. It's a make or break appointment!'

On their way to the Taj Hotel at Mansingh Road, Bhaskaran was constantly rubbing his stubble, as if to stimulate his jaw. Som asked him a thousand questions on where they were going and why. The only reply he got was, 'I have an excellent business idea. We are going to meet some people who will fund the plan.'

Som was dressed in business formals but not in a suit. The way Bhaskaran sprang up on him, he had no time to brush up his jacket either. So every now and then, he would pull at his cuffs, trying to straighten out the creases on his white shirt.

When they reached their destination, it started pouring. 'See, good omen!' said Bhaskaran.

They ran for the reception and took the elevators. When they had disembarked at the top floor, Som was surprised to see a banner that read: Kickstart Ventures Welcomes Semi-finalists of Business Ideas Contest.

'What on earth is going on? I thought you said they would fund your plan. You are just a semi-finalist in a contest!' yelled Som.

'Quiet now,' said Bhaskaran. 'I will explain everything. Now come, we are two minutes late.'

The lady at the desk was pleasing in manners and etiquette. Without a fuss, she led the boys to the last room down a narrow corridor. Inside were seated five middle-aged gentlemen of various nationalities, looking thoroughly amused. *They've already had their share of entertainment this afternoon*, Som thought.

As they shook hands and sat down, Som could see that while two of them were Indians, two looked Chinese and one a Caucasian. The tallest, an Indian, spoke, 'My name is Atul Bindal, I am the MD of Kickstart Ventures, and here are my partners – Bill Mason, Chin Lee, Robert Cheng, and Ashish Saklani. It's nice to see you, Mr Bhaskaran, and we look forward to your business presentation.'

'Almost every adult human hopes to get married some day,' Bhaskaran began to speak. Som did not bat an eyelid.

Bhaskaran continued, 'Many marriages are a consequence of romance or acquaintance. Some are borne out of personal references. And the rest are arranged through public advertisement. The ₹ 5,000 crore organised matrimonial services industry in India caters to two crore individuals per annum, and is led by several websites offering profiles of marriageable individuals for a fee. However, as far as the rate of response is concerned, newspaper ads seem to generate more initial interest, maybe because a photograph of the prospective bride or groom is not immediately available for rejection.'

Atul Bindal chuckled.

'The main drawback of the matrimonial portals is that while they offer a vast database with photographs and horoscopes, it is extremely difficult to trust the information posted online and sieve through thousands of profiles to identify that "one" suitable prospect. Also, candidates are often embarrassed to find themselves posted for years on the web. Then there is the added nuisance of casual fun-seekers and sexual predators posing as interested parties on the chat facility provided.'

Som felt a shiver run down his spine. He did not have a good feeling about this business.

But Bhaskaran was going great guns. 'Despite there being at least three different platforms for matrimonial services in India, the sector is still not very professional in terms of range or scope of services. The key thing here is that while "matching" profiles, no logic or rationale is considered apart from horoscope checks. Therefore, the "success" rate of these marriages is also under question.

'Herein lies the opportunity of establishing a matrimonial agency that offers personalised matchmaking services based on logical methodologies that assure stability in marriages,' he asserted.

There was pin-drop silence in the room. 'What is the USP of your business idea?' asked Atul.

Bhaskaran smiled knowledgeably. 'My company, Matchmakers Inc, will be India's first matrimonial services agency providing personalised and customised search and matchmaking services, enabled by IT and based on proven principles of psychology, medicine, and astrology.'

Bill Jason looked confused. 'And what is the Logic Match process all about?'

Bhaskaran continued to wax eloquent, 'You see, every member will be required to fill up a computerised profile questionnaire about personal data, education, habits and occupation, family background, and general parameters to be chosen while searching for a life partner. Additionally, a psychologist will interview the member and cross-check the details filled in the profile questionnaire. The member is then taken to the agency doctor who fills a computerised health check report. In the meantime, the agency counsellor will generate a computerised Star Check report by feeding in birth information of the member. The Logic Match process will shortlist all matching Intelligent Profiles and generate Compatibility Index scores against each of them. Logic Match reports with matches having overall CI scores of more than fifty per cent will be generated for each member once every month,' he concluded.

'Is that all?' asked Robert Cheng.

'We have more services,' clarified Bhaskaran. 'For couples contemplating divorce, the Logic Match process will be applied for post-marital counselling for a one-time fee. We will also provide free value-added and partner recommendatory services for loans, insurance, event management, and travel.'

Som was shifting about nervously in his seat.

Ashish Saklani cleared his throat and asked in a sarcastic tone, 'How will *you* know which marriages will work and which ones will not?'

'Not me, Sir,' said Bhaskaran. 'The *software* will know, Sir. It will not match a boisterous guy with a reserved girl. It will not match a B-positive with an A-negative person. It will not recommend that a *Shakespeare* fan marry a Tom & Jerry one. And then, of course, there's the mandatory horoscope match.'

'What is your target segment?' asked Ashish.

'Urban marriageable Hindu, Sikh, Christian, Buddhist, and Jain youth, including singles, divorcees, and widows. We cannot serve gays and transvestites yet under the law. All should be educated and English speaking, Sec A and Sec B only,' Bhaskaran submitted.

'OK, can I have a look at your financials?' Atul asked.

'Sure,' Bhaskaran said, pulling out a soggy white paper from his pocket. 'Here it is.'

'Projected Financials

Estimated new Members per Branch per month in Year 1 – Around 200

Fees per Member – ₹ 11,000

Revenue per Branch per month – ₹ 22,00,000 or ₹ 2.64 crore per annum

Annual projected turnover with 5 Branches – ₹ 13.20 crore for the 1st year

Capital Expenditure for 5 Branches – ₹ 90 lakh for 1st year

IT Hardware – 50 lakh
IT Software and patented software Logic Match programme – 10 lakh
Furniture and Furnishings and Electricals – 10 lakh
5 Company Cars – 20 lakh
Operating Expenses per annum for 5 Branches for the 1st year – ₹17.40 crore
Salaries for HO employees – 2 crore
Salaries for Branch Employees and Vendor Contracts – 3 crore
Rentals – 2 crore
Electricity and Phone Bills – 15 lakh
Advertising and Marketing expenses – 10 crore
Misc – 25 lakh
Total expenses – ₹18.30 crore in Year 1
Cash Break-even in middle of Year 2'

Atul read aloud the items on the paper.

Som's head was spinning wildly like a wheel. Bhaskaran had just made him the CEO of a multi-crore business.

Bill Jason broke the silence. 'Well, I still have a remaining question, and I wonder if that's the most important question here. I can understand the part about matching blood group and medical history. I also see the point about checking that partners are comfortable with each others' lifestyle. But how do you match personalities? To say that both partners have to be quiet and peace-loving is clichéd. I mean, how can you say that Type A will get along well with Type B personalities and so on? It sounds so much like *Linda Goodman's Love Signs*. My wife is a Piscean and I am a Scorpio but we can't agree on one thing under the sun for God's sake!'

The entire room burst into laughter.

Bhaskaran looked to Som and said, 'Why don't you explain the concept, Mr CEO?'

The heavens fell on Som. He went completely blank for a few seconds. And then, gathering his wits, he spoke slowly.

'Well, Mr Jason, we are not talking about Linda Goodman here. We are referring to Swiss psychiatrist Carl Gustav Jung's Theory of Personality Types which classifies all humans broadly into four basic personality types. This theory was further evolved by Katharine and Isabel Briggs to arrive at sixteen personality types.

'The theory contends that an individual is either primarily extroverted or introverted; sensing or intuitive; thinking or feeling; and judging or perceiving. The possible combinations of the basic preferences form sixteen different personality types. This does not mean that all individuals will fall strictly into one category or another. However, we can identify our natural preferences, and learn about our natural strengths and weaknesses in that context.

'Learning about our personality type helps us understand why we face certain situations easily and struggle with others. Learning about other people's personality types helps us understand how they perceive and judge the world, and what makes them comfortable. With that knowledge, one knows if sailing on the same boat is possible with a prospective partner.'

'Well put.' Ashish Saklani removed a card from his wallet and handed over to Som. 'Call me tomorrow.'

Bhaskaran was a bit confused.

Atul Bindal looked at Bhaskar and summarised. 'You see, our primary assessment is that your business is risky and capital intensive. But we'll get back to you after a detailed discussion.'

On the way back, Bhaskaran asked Som, 'Where did you get that personality theory lecture from?'

'Psychology books in College Street, Kolkata. You had left me no choice. What a rascal you are! Making up a business plan in your mind,' said Som angrily.

Bhaskaran teased Som, 'Dada, rasogolla!'

Chapter 6

The Apprentice

Kenny shut the door behind him as he left for work early that morning.

He would move to Mumbai on the first day of July, and that is when Som would be rendered homeless.

Presently, Som was spread on the bed with legs stretched apart, hands holding the morning newspaper very close to his face. He ran his eyes over the headlines – demonstrations in Srinagar, murders in South Delhi, and the threat of drought looming large.

Disgusted, he pulled the 'Dilli Now' supplement. It had Bollywood stars on the front page, campus updates on page two, socialites and cricketers on page three, and semi-nude Hollywood celebrities over the remaining pages.

J. Lo. Wants to Have a Baby, screamed one news item. The famous rock star was seen crouching on her knees, sticking her tongue out as if to catch a fly. In another item, a teenage acting sensation was reported to have changed her boyfriend last weekend.

Som wondered when was the last time he had read or seen something on freedom fighters, scientists, musicians, or stage artists.

Exasperated, he threw the paper on the floor.

And then he remembered that his cellphone had run out of balance and ma would be worried if she called and heard a 'this number is temporarily unavailable' message. He also remembered Ashish Saklani asking him to call during the day.

Som quickly put on his jeans and T-shirt, and went down to the grocer outside the housing society.

There was a long line of customers waiting at Rattan's shop. Some waited for eggs and bread, others for milk, and still others for cigarettes and paan. Som spotted their maid, Reshma, standing at one end, talking agitatedly to someone on the landline.

'*Humse bahut badi galti hoi rahi, tum topi kahe nahin pehnat ho raat ma?*' she asked someone.

Som wondered why anyone should wear a cap at all at night. And then, the metaphor struck him hard. Realising Reshma might be carrying an illegitimate child, he panicked. *What if she blames Kenny or Som as the father?* The boys were soft targets and the proof of their innocence would not come forth before nine months anyway. By then, Ram Mukherjee would behead his son.

'Rattan bhaiyya,' screamed Som, 'please recharge my phone for two hundred bucks. You have the number in the register. Take this money.'

Reshma was startled and looked back at Som. But he had moved around swiftly and was taking giant, awkward strides back to his apartment.

Shortly after Som reached home, the doorbell rang.

Reshma had come to sweep the floor and wash the dishes.

On other days, Som hardly noticed her but today, she seemed to be hovering all around him, swaying her hips suggestively to the song on the radio – '*Kaanta Lagaa....*' Som was getting very scared and did not know what to do.

In a flash, he visualised dozens of men beating him with sandals, coaxing him to marry Reshma.

Just then, the cellphone came to life.

'Bhaskaran, what's up? You got funding for your marriage agency? No? Then what? What? Saklani has called us? But when did you call him? His card is with me, or did you steal it? Rascal!'

Som put the phone down. 'Enough, behanji. It's enough for today. I got to go out quickly. You come again tomorrow,' he said to Reshma.

As the maid left somewhat reluctantly, Som heaved a sigh of relief.

THERE WERE A handful of offices functioning from a multi-storey residential building at Hailey Road in Central Delhi. Bhaskaran and Som walked into one of them.

Ashish Saklani was very happy to see Som. He was short and stout, and always wore a proud expression on his face.

'Look, I heard what you guys presented yesterday to Kickstart Ventures. And I know that your proposal is too risky to fund. But there is something I can offer you in my private capacity. I own this public relations firm which is now exactly one month old. I have named it "Thinking Caps". We are currently putting together a team of talented, smart people like you to service our clients and also build media contacts,' he said.

Som felt eternally grateful to all the Gods of all religions.

'My offer to you both is simple,' Ashish continued, 'meet my talent acquisition head in the next room and understand your roles. If all goes well, I will hire you both as apprentices for twenty grands a month for the next six months. Depending on how you perform, I will sign your confirmation letters on renewed terms.'

'Thank you, Sir,' said a thrilled Som. Bhaskaran just smiled.

Ashish Saklani smiled back and rose to greet them off.

In the next room, a man was typing on his computer. His back was towards the door where Som and Bhaskaran stood quietly.

'Excuse me, Sir. Mr Saklani asked us to meet you,' Som pleaded.

'Oh well, if *captain* has sent you, I will meet you,' said the man and revolved around to face the boys.

Som felt a great stirring inside him. His heart leapt with joy.

'Professor Vibhas Pandey of Hindu College? Do you recognise me, Sir?'

The three had a great lunch. Soon, empty boxes of pizza and bottles of cola lay strewn across Dr Pandey's table.

The ex-professor began narrating to Som how his life had changed in the past one year since they both had met in the Rajdhani Express from Kolkata to Delhi.

'As I had told you then, Som, it has always been important for me to examine my life from the point of view of whether it is of any larger significance. While I would like to believe that I was a good teacher at college, I was increasingly unsure about what my students did with the knowledge of history that I imparted to them. And one day, it dawned upon me that this generation is no longer interested. A boy of your age once stood up in class and asked me why they should learn about Jinnah, Nehru, and pre-partition riots when the world has moved ahead so much. I asked him what part of history would interest him then. The boy simply had no answer,' said Dr Pandey.

Bhaskaran was amused for some reason.

Som asked, 'But these guys enrolled for History classes. It's part of their curriculum, isn't it?'

'Yes and no,' replied Dr Pandey. 'You see,' he continued, 'these days, the name of the college is bigger than the degree itself. It is a status symbol for some people. So they will take up any course available in their preferred college, only to change the course in the second year or suffer the lectures somehow.'

'That's sad if you study just for the sake of it,' sighed Som.

'Yes, and I realised I could no longer go on as a mere facilitator for degree-seekers. Ashish Saklani is a friend's acquaintance. He was looking for a good, knowledge-enabled team for Thinking Caps and I thought it is here where I could make a difference. If I understand correctly, PR is the art and science of nurturing trust and goodwill between people and organisations, and it needs attitude, sensitivity, and learning.

'Since Ashish has already selected you both, he has made my job easy. Of course, I also happen to know what Som is made up of so that helps too,' he smiled.

'Look boys, I have been interviewing young people for the last four days now, and have shortlisted many of them already for specific roles. There are exactly two positions that are yet to be filled, but I'm afraid they are not within the same team. I hope that's not a problem?' asked Dr Pandey.

'No, Sir,' replied Bhaskaran. 'We are happy to get our daily bread and help in creating goodwill between people and organisations.'

Som and Dr Pandey broke into a laugh.

'Good then,' remarked the professor. 'I will put you, Som, in the client servicing team, under Santosh Yadav. He is a capable leader and has over ten years of experience in public affairs. He has also worked as a journalist for some time. I think you will like him.'

Turning to Bhaskaran, he said, 'And you, Bhaskaran, will assist Raghu Pillai in the media relations team. This team is responsible for coordinating with the press on behalf of our clients on a daily basis. As far as delivery is concerned, the buck stops at Raghu's desk. There is nothing more satisfying to the client than a balanced, well-presented article in the press.

'You both will be apprentices for six months with a fixed stipend. After that, you will be confirmed in the right grade on the basis of your aptitude and performance.'

The two boys looked at each other. Bhaskaran winked at Som.

While completing joining formalities, Som prayed that the experience he had at Pink Dot Advertising would not be repeated. He had faith in Dr Vibhas Pandey's judgement, and if the professor had staked his reputation and career, then Thinking Caps could just not be another blot.

IN THE EVENING, Kenny and Som sat together.

'Kenny, now that I got a job, I need a house after you are gone. I was wondering if the landlord would let me continue here if I got another room-mate and paid the rent,' said Som.

'Why, that should be possible,' said Kenny. 'Can you pay ten thousand as rent?'

'Yes, if I get a room-mate,' replied Som.

'OK, you leave that to me, and now let's jam up for old time sakes.' Kenny was in high spirits. Shortly afterwards, he was strumming merrily on his guitar while Som sang '*the summer of 69....*'

They played and sang for hours that evening. After some Western numbers, they switched to popular Bollywood music. Som was not a singer but had a good grip on scale and tune. Kenny indulged him lovingly, just to enliven his otherwise solo practice.

'I don't understand or follow Hindi music that much, but if you listen to the radio these days, a lot of them are using rock beats, isn't it?' asked Kenny.

'Oh yes, we are learning from each other. Traditionally, Western music uses the harmony principle, using instruments to produce harmonious tones, while Hindi music has been about rhythm and melody,' said Som.

Talking about the diverse forms of music, the boys felt very hungry. They made omelettes and then hit the bed.

'Reshma is pregnant,' announced Som.

Kenny jumped up, startled. 'Is that why you are so happy today? I thought you had better taste.'

'Of course I do. I was just shocked that you preferred her over Aparna.'

Kenny took his pillow and smacked it at Som's face. The latter got up and pushed Kenny to the floor and tried to strangulate him. After a prolonged pillow fight, they finally called it a truce.

'No, this is serious, Som,' said a panting Kenny. 'With me gone, I don't want you in any mess. Fire her after I'm out next week.

'And yes, ask her the name of the father. I'm just curious. It could be Birjoo, the gardener, or Sher Singh, the gatekeeper.'

'I have better things to do in life,' said Som.

SANTOSH YADAV WAS waiting in the meeting room. The entire client servicing team had assembled for a briefing session. Exhausted after last night's mock fight, Som had forgotten to set the alarm and had woken up well past eight in the morning.

'You must be Somashish Mukherjee,' said Santosh when he saw the door open slightly.

'Come in, please.'

'Sorry for being late, actually I was ...' Som started to offer an apology.

'It's OK, first day of work. You are being let off today. Please be on time tomorrow,' said Santosh. 'By the way, here are your colleagues. Let me introduce them to you.'

Som waved his hand to say hello to all present in the room. There were four others apart from Santosh – two young men and two young ladies. All of them looked smart and bright.

'Seated on my left are Ejaz Ahmed, senior consultant, and his teammate, Tanya Sachdev. They take care of the lifestyle and entertainment clients.'

Ejaz was smartly dressed in a crisp white shirt and green tie. He smiled at Som. Tanya wore a cream business shirt, and was nibbling a pencil.

'Towards my right is senior consultant, Prem Rawat, and junior consultant, Payal Mehra. They together manage the FMCG and automotives portfolio,' continued Santosh.

Prem was in jeans and a T-shirt for some reason. He looked at Som but did not smile. Payal was seated right next to Som and stretched out her hand to him. She had a glowing, fair complexion and long, dark brown hair. Her round eyes were brown and shone brightly under the white light. 'How do you do,' Som said and shook her hand.

'Guys, Som will work with me directly for some time until further notice. In effect, it means that he will work alone most of the time since I am going to be rarely available. He will handle all corporate clients and any new wins in healthcare and insurance,' announced Santosh.

Som's heart skipped a beat. He was being thrown into a sea, all alone. *Perfect recipe for disaster*, he thought.

'By the way, Som, we just lost our first healthcare client,' informed Santosh. 'There is this journalist, Muthukumaran, who was expecting VIP treatment for his grandfather at Phoolchand Hospital. We didn't offer him any discounts or freebies. So, instead of reporting on their latest 4-D CT scan machine, he did a story on MRI facilities at a competing hospital. I told the client that there are only a handful of journos covering the healthcare beat and they need to be treated with care, but we got the boot.'

'You will not have it easy, Som. I promise,' Santosh warned, smiling.

It struck Som that this Muthukumaran was none other than his IIMC batchmate and class topper. *He shouldn't be so difficult to manage*, Som thought.

Santosh then went on to take the team through a PowerPoint presentation depicting the main clients of the agency, key issues, deliverables, and contract clauses. A planning chart was created for the following week and everybody was asked to stick a print-out on their work stations.

By noon, the briefing ended.

Ejaz and Prem huddled into a corner with Santosh. Payal and Tanya led the way out. 'I can't describe how cute he was,' Payal was telling Tanya. 'The guy had the sexiest butt I have ever seen!' she said.

Som, who was following them, was flabbergasted. Back in Kolkata, he had heard girls describing boys as tall and handsome but none had ever commented on a guy's assets!

'If this is the way they would talk here, I will surely not have it easy,' he mused.

The hallway had sixteen modular work stations in a four by four arrangement. Som stood wondering for a while and then settled for a seat in the far corner that overlooked the whole office. Soon enough, Raghu Pillai came out of an adjacent meeting room with Bhaskaran and two other girls in tow.

Raghu looked drugged and dazed while Bhaskaran was grinning from ear to ear. The girls in his team wore a heavy make-up and carried designer bags. It was difficult to tell if they were fake, but Som didn't hazard a guess.

Bhaskaran took pity on Som and picked a seat nearby, for moral support. The first thing he did was to turn his computer in a way that others could not see the monitor. His team members sat futher down the hall, near the office entrance.

Som folded his palms in prayer before switching on the computer. As it blinked to life, Santosh walked over with a smile.

'I have your first assignment up already, Som. It's a Saturday tomorrow but there is some business which you can treat as pleasure. You have to escort two guests to Rishikesh for a religious conclave, sponsored by the K Corp Foundation. Once there, you have to invite some local photographers to cover the conference. All expenses will be borne by K Corp. Take a five thousand advance from Dr Pandey. I will arrange for a taxi to pick you up in the morning. Game?'

Som leapt up at the thought. Rishikesh sounded exotic and would be his first trip out of Delhi.

'I would go even if I had a choice,' said Som. Santosh just grinned.

Chapter 7

A River of Thoughts

Just as Santosh had instructed, Som reached the residence of Vishambhar Narain Dutt in Kohat Enclave in North Delhi at half past eleven in the morning.

He looked around at the neighbourhood of two-storey garden houses, and wondered why the locality was named after a Pakistani town. The taxi driver climbed out of the Ambassador in impatience. After all, he had a six-hour drive to Rishikesh ahead of him.

A tiny boy in soiled vest and pants answered the bell. Upon hearing Vishambhar's name, he signalled to Som to come in and be seated. 'Poor thing,' Som thought, 'must be hardly getting anything to eat.'

The living room was cramped and looked more like a publishing house. Stacks of paper and magazines lay bound on the floor. Bookshelves occupied most of the space around him, and there were several calendars and Sanskrit posters hanging from the walls. On one of the walls, Som noticed a giant photograph of a bearded swami blessing a man in a white kurta-pyjama. A thick necklace of rudraksha beads hung from the neck of the man, apparently a disciple.

On the table in front of him lay several copies of *Tantra Mantra Monthly* magazine. Som had neither seen nor ever heard of the magazine. A particular article on 'how to earn riches through the Swarna Prabha Yakshini' drew his attention. If there were indeed such shortcuts to success, Bhaskaran would take them all, he thought.

'Mr Mukherjee?' spoke a voice from behind him.

As Som turned around, a tall, dark man emerged from behind the dusty Jaipuri curtains. It did not take long to recognise him as the grateful disciple in the giant photo.

'Namaste, Mr Dutt,' said Som, joining his palms together.

'I am from K Corp's PR agency. Santosh Yadav sent me to escort you to Rishikesh,' he said.

'Yes, of course. Let me just pack my Liv-52 capsules and I am ready to go!' said Vishambhar.

Som nodded his head sideways in practiced agreement as Vishambhar adjusted the silken scarf around his neck, careful not to entangle it in the rudraksha maala. He was dressed in a pristine white kurta-pyjama and wore black leather sandals.

After several minutes of packing and unpacking his shoulderbag, Vishambhar was finally ready to move. As they came out of the door, the driver muttered a few curses under his breath.

Soon, the white Ambassador was dodging its way down the Ring Road, towards Lajpat Nagar. Som sat beside the driver while Vishambhar was spread on the rear seat in regal splendour.

'Are we picking up someone else?' Vishambhar asked.

'Yes,' said Som. 'We will be joined by Madam Nargis Kaul from Srinagar. She is also here to participate in the all-faith meeting in Rishikesh.'

'Kashmir, that sounds great!' Vishambhar sounded elated for some reason.

For the next hour or so, Vishambhar talked about his adventures in Kashmir during the Amarnath Yatra of 1999. It was quite an eventful journey, if he was to be believed. He had rare sightings of *apsaras* or heavenly nymphs dancing on rocky hills at Pahalgam, and had even touched the feet of a vanishing *siddha* at Anantanag.

'So, what do these heavenly bodies do when they are not playing, err ... interacting with humans?' asked a bemused Som. The driver coughed.

'You see, Mukherjee, these ethereal beings do not have to work in a PR agency or publish magazines like me to earn a living. They exist because they do not die. They cannot die. So sometimes they play among themselves, joke around, fly here and there, and help people like us. They get a great ego-trip after helping us. We are like helpless toys to them. But there are ways in which man can attract them and use them to obtain boons and gifts. My latest issue of *Tantra Mantra Monthly* goes deep into the technique of using such beings to our advantage,' replied Vishambhar.

'Yes, I saw an article about Swarna Prabha Yakshini in your magazine. Is she one of them?' asked Som.

Vishambhar suddenly became silent, as if in holy reverence.

'It is not a theory but an actual experience that I had in the Kumaon Himalayas. I was very young then, practicing austerities as instructed by my guruji, living on nothing but fruits and milk, and wearing only tree barks,' he said.

Som felt a great story coming. The taxi was stuck in a jam at Naraina and only angels could deliver them. *Not a bad timing*, he thought.

Vishambhar continued in a sombre tone, scratching his short moustache. 'So, there I was in the freezing cold, all by myself, doing chantings and preparing offerings all day. When no benefit was forthcoming even after the eleventh day, I lost all hope. I decided to come back to Delhi and find some other guru.

'It was a moonless night and I lay tired on the mud floor of the hut I had built for myself. Some kitten was crying in the distance. After some time, the crying stopped and I heard the distinct sound of metal. I remembered that there was some milk left in the saucepan and inferred that the cat must have found it.

'As I pushed out my right hand to ward off the cat, it landed on something solid and warm. I instinctively grabbed hold of the shaft-like thing only to realise it was human skin!' Vishambhar was visibly excited.

'Even now my hair stands on their end when I think of the moment. I almost froze to death then. Very slowly, I explored the thing further. As I moved my palm upwards, it was clear that my hand was on a female thigh.'

The driver suddenly applied the brakes and the taxi screeched to a halt.

'What happened?' asked Som, jolted out of concentration.

'Cat, Sir,' the driver replied, pointing to a large black pussycat that had jumped over the road fencing.

They were now at Moti Bagh and still had about twenty minutes to cover.

'Drive carefully or you'll have us all dead. A cat has nine lives but you have only one,' scolded Vishambhar. Taking a deep breath, he continued, 'I tell you Mukherjee, my heart was in my mouth. I just could not believe that there was a lady in my hut in the middle of the night. I got up like a snake and stared hard to figure out who or what she was.

'I could only make out her outline in the dark but it was very clear that she was wearing only gold ornaments, nothing else. When I asked her name, she only giggled and said she was my eternal servant. She wanted to sit in my lap and give me all her celestial jewellery.'

'And then?' Som asked.

'And then I committed the biggest mistake of my life,' replied Vishambhar. 'I was scared that she was a witch who would kill me, so I cast the *Bagalamukhi* spell on her. She got so enraged that she spewed litres of blood on me.

'The next morning, I fainted and fell into the river and was found a mile away by a sadhu, who saved my life. However, I got jaundice and have to pop these Liv-52 pills even to this day,' concluded Vishambhar.

'She was a *pucca chudail,* Sir,' butted in the driver. 'We have lots of them in Gorakhpur. They will follow you around in the evening when you go to relieve yourself in the fields, asking *shall I come, shall I come*? If, by any chance, a man agrees, then he has had it. The witch will possess him and kill everyone else who comes near him.'

Som felt nauseous.

'Now I know the difference between a witch, *yakshini* and *yogini,*' said Vishambhar. 'And I can guide people like you, Som. She will not return to me ever but you can lure her easily.'

Som did not know what to say. 'I think we are there already,' he managed to feebly mumble.

NARGIS KAUL WAS waiting for them in the balcony of her sister's house in E-Block, Lajpat Nagar. She stood up as she saw the white Ambassador approach. Som rolled down the window glass to tally the address with the note on his cellphone.

He noticed a plump lady, probably in her fifties, staring at him from behind the iron gate.

'It must be her,' he thought.

'You got the wrong house,' asserted Vishambhar from the rear seat.

'Are you Somashish Mukherjee?' yelled the lady.

It was already forty minutes past one when the trio entered a popular Chinese restaurant in New Friends Colony for lunch. Som offered his guests a variety of options to choose from, but Nargis and Vishambhar could not agree on any common item. So they ended up ordering six different dishes.

The taxi crossed the Hindon river in Ghaziabad at four in the evening and Som got really worried that they would not be able to cross the Ganga in Rishikesh by car, as Santosh had warned. So they decided not to break the journey at Khatauli but carry on straight ahead to their destination.

After a while, both Nargis and Vishambhar fell fast asleep.

Som looked out of the window on his left. He could see endless fields of sugarcane right upto the horizon. There were tubewells jetting out water into concrete tanks, and farm boys were washing themselves in the stream.

In the fading light of the evening, Som's mind drifted into the distant past. He remembered the college excursion to Shantiniketan, the Saal trees on both sides of the road, and the wind playing with Chandni's long, black hair.

She was sitting with Garima on the right side of the bus while Som and Basu sat in a row ahead on the left. A group of students was singing popular Hindi and Bengali film songs.

'*Zindagi ek safar hai suhana...*' yodled Basu.

Every now and then, Basu would turn back to wink at or air-kiss Garima, who returned the gesture each time. Som had felt greatly embarrassed at Basu's antics and when Basu threw a paper dart at Garima, Som turned in horror to see it land on Chandni's face.

Garima was busy chatting with a friend behind her and Basu's dart had obviously missed its target. The offender quickly hid his face, leaving Som gaping at Chandni.

Chandni picked up the dart and read 'I love you'. She looked up at Som and had almost let out a smile when Basu reared his head to apologise. 'Sorry, it was for Garima,' he said.

The most unlikely of all love stories was nipped in the bud.

'Are you also sleeping, Sir?' the driver jolted Som back to the present.

'No,' replied Som. 'I was just thinking.'

'About your family? Wife, Sir?'

'No, I am not married yet,' said Som.

'Oh yes, Sir. I forgot. Only villagers like us get married early. They say that a man loses his head if he is not married off in time. The same applies to women too. Now look at what happened last month. A police inspector in our village had this beautiful daughter whom he would not wed to this good-for-nothing fellow. Both were madly in love, like elephants in *musth*. One day, she ran away with him. Now the wretched couple lives in Delhi, constantly quarrelling over money and blaming each other. What is the use of such a marriage, Sir?'

'Yes, no use,' Som solemnly agreed.

'What is your name, driver?' he asked.

'My name is Sunil, Sir.'

Som could not quite fathom the moral of the story. Was it wrong to fall in love or to marry in love? Which was the bigger crime of the two?

'Sunil bhaiya, please stop at Khatauli for a minute,' commanded Nargis.

Som did not realise that his guests had woken up and were eavesdropping.

'Love need not turn into marriage always. But when it can, one should treasure it,' said Nargis.

When the driver pulled over, they all got off to refresh themselves. 'I knew you cannot drive at a stretch with an old lady in tow,' complained Vishambhar. 'Now we'll reach Rishikesh past midnight.'

When the journey resumed, Nargis offered them paan. She looked rested and relieved as she chewed on it, maintaining a steady gaze over the road ahead.

'So where in Srinagar do you reside, Madam?' asked Vishambhar. 'I know the city like the back of my palm.'

'Sorry to disappoint you, Vishambhar, but I live in New Jersey, US,' said Nargis. There was a wry smile in the corner of her lips, concealed by the locks of silver hair that fell around her chubby face in a curve.

Vishambhar fell back in the seat as if stung by a scorpion.

'Som informed me that you were from Srinagar. That is why I was asking,' he protested.

'Sure, I am from Srinagar. I was born there as Nargis Bano and migrated to the States in 1970 with my family. That is where

I met Dr Kaul. He was a NASA scientist, you see. Our families were opposed to the marriage and when he could not bear the pain any more, he simply walked off a cliff.'

There was stoic silence.

'But you are Nargis Kaul, Madam.' Som was a bit surprised.

'Yes, death could not separate us. After I got my American citizenship, I changed my surname to Kaul. That's the least I could do for that great soul.'

'Appreciate your sentiments. But Doctor Kaul was not right in committing suicide. A man who takes that path is once again made to suffer the same predicament in the next life. And he is reborn after a period of prolonged torture and agony. There is no escape from the laws of karma,' asserted Vishambhar.

'That is absolute nonsense. Doctor Kaul ended his life because his task in this world was finished. He still sends me inspiring messages from the other world, and I get answers to all my questions. I don't subscribe to any formal religion. The Lord above alone is my religion.'

The road had narrowed down as the taxi approached Roorkee. The air was becoming colder and the traffic from the opposite direction blinded them.

'Dr Kaul says that we are not alone in this world. Even as we speak, hundreds of our friends from distant galaxies are silently cleaning up green house gases from the atmosphere and replenishing the ozone layer. If it were not for them, there would be a catastrophe very soon,' revealed Nargis.

'You mean the yakshas and gandharvas? Yes, they do help but not always. They act thus only when there is a command from heaven or a *havan* is ritually performed.' Vishambhar had his own theory.

'Call them whatever,' said Nargis. 'The fact is that UFOs are a reality, brutally suppressed by the US Government and NATO countries. Because the aliens are so powerful and intelligent beyond compare, poor countries can easily use them to defeat American hegemony. That's precisely what the Pentagon does not want. They try to block every chance of inter-species interaction, even firing rockets at UFO spaceships!'

Vishambhar was perplexed and did not know what to say.

'Did Dr Kaul tell you all this, Nargisji?' asked Som.

'Yes. He told me that there are thousands of inhabited planets in the Milky Way itself. But not all beings are able to travel to our planet yet. Those who visit us, are of the most evolved kind. They are mentally so evolved that they are beyond greed, jealousy, and anger. They know what they need, how much they need, and share everything among themselves.'

Som had heard about suspected UFO sightings in Himachal Pradesh and Uttaranchal but never believed the stories. Now he was listening to tales that sounded straight from sci-fi books.

'We could be progressive like the aliens too, only if we could control our population,' he said.

'You can be assured that your Government is working very hard, indeed, to control the population. Your daily dose of iodised salt reduces male fertility over a period of time. There is no better birth control method than this. Silent and effective,' summarised Nargis.

Som didn't believe in the salt conspiracy. He wondered how Nargis had heard so much of the weird stuff.

Vishambhar was at great unease. He rolled down the window and pointed to a cluster of bright lights in the distance. 'Look, we are approaching Haridwar,' he announced.

Som's mind was a whirlpool of thoughts as they passed by Har-ki-Pauri. Caught between celestials and aliens on the one hand and conspiring politicians on the other, he was unsure of what life meant to him and where he was headed. And what was this job that landed him on a pilgrimage?

It was eleven in the night when the group finally reached Ram Jhoola in Rishikesh. They had to park the taxi on this side of the river and walk across the old suspended footbridge to the other side.

Som was awestruck as he looked at the water beneath. It was placid and magnificent, vast and loving, like a mother who had stopped by to kiss her children goodnight.

Som forgot all his worries and surrendered to the magical tranquility of the place. Cow bells rang out somewhere nearby.

If he had to spend his entire life here at Rishikesh, he was now ready to do so.

Chapter 8

Crisis

Santosh Yadav looked bright and cheerful on Tuesday morning.

'Guys, I'd like you to applaud Somashish here,' he announced.

'The boy went to Rishikesh on Saturday with two eccentric characters – one a tantric and the other a spirit medium. Not only did he survive the ordeal but also managed to arrange some good photo opportunities for the all-faith meeting sponsored by K Corp Foundation.'

Holding aloft a Hindi newspaper, Santosh said, 'Here is the photo of Rattan Kathuria, Chairman of K Corp. Look how he is flanked by orange, cream, white, and green robes. See how happy he looks!'

Ejaz, Tania, Prem, and Payal clapped aloud.

'What is Kathuria upto? Taking retirement or something?' Prem enquired.

'Far from that,' clarified Santosh. 'He will make it big. Thanks to his secular image, he will get a ticket to contest the parliamentary elections from any mainstream political party. Even if he doesn't win an election, an entry to the upper house is guaranteed. Parties need industrialists as much as the latter need them. He could make a good Union Minister for Commerce and Industry.'

Eyebrows were raised in the room. Tania guffawed. Som felt like an accomplice in a great robbery.

'OK, now give me your team reports one by one. Ejaz?' said Santosh.

Ejaz cleared his voice. 'Well, we got some good press coverage for Bhatia Productions' next release, *Love in California*. *Bharat Times* has rated the movie with four stars, although we were not involved and don't take credit for such paid reviews.'

'Tonight, Tania and I are all set to go to Mumbai for the fashion week. Our apparel manufacturing client, X-tinction, will be showcasing their winter collection there,' he said.

'Who are the designers this year?' asked Santosh.

'Remo D'souza and Cauvery Nair,' replied Ejaz.

Santosh turned to Tanya. 'What do the designs look like, Tanya, and who'll wear them?'

Tanya dropped the pencil she was fiddling with and removed her thick-rimmed spectacles. Som noticed that her eyes were beautiful, though they looked very sad all the time. 'Not like Chandni's eyes,' he thought.

'The clothes are very avant garde and upmarket. The two designers have used nylon, fake leather, polyester, and jute apart from cotton and silk. The colours are gothic shades of blacks, greys, and browns. The models they will use include actor Archana Singh and Rohit Kapoor, so the appeal will be mainly to the party circuit.'

'Have you taken samples and photos for the lifestyle magazines and page three slots?' demanded Santosh in an unusually stern tone.

Tanya was surprised. She had no answer and just looked at Ejaz for a clue.

'Don't need them now,' said Ejaz. 'Once we get to Mumbai, we'll develop the press kits. Or do you want to pay for excess baggage, Santosh?'

Santosh smiled.

'Good then, Prem Rawat?'

'I would rather let Payal talk,' said Prem. 'I was out on leave most of the last week. My father is sick in Nainital.'

'What exactly happened?' Santosh was concerned.

'Pneumonia. He went to Kasauni and walked in the snow,' regretted Prem.

'Don't worry, Prem, he'll be fine,' remarked Payal, placing a hand on his shoulder. Everybody nodded.

'Actually, while Prem was away, I was busy organising a media visit to the New Foods factory in Sonepat. They have this new line of chocolate drinks and health foods that are manufactured in the state-of-the-art plant imported from Munich. We showed the journalists how buffalo milk is collected at the community centres, processed, and then converted into finished products.'

'Which journalists did you take? The ones who cover product launches?' asked Ejaz.

'No,' said Payal. 'We took the features guys who write on new-age foods and health topics. They will continue to write about it in several articles.'

'Really smart girl,' praised Santosh.

'I'm sorry but why buffalo milk? Isn't cow milk healthier?' asked Som.

Payal cracked up. 'It doesn't matter, Som,' she said. 'After processing, the extra fat is removed anyways.' She was still laughing.

Som wondered why Payal was in splits.

Just then, the door banged open. Raghu Pillai entered with Bhaskaran and two girls. Som noticed the high heels.

Bhaskaran was grinning from ear to ear.

'Boss, there is a crisis,' said a trembled Raghu. His eyes were bloodshot, and he seemed baffled.

'I need blood. Lots of it ...' he cried. 'The deputy editor of *Times Today* is dying of dengue. Guys, who is B-positive here?'

Everybody except Santosh, Som, and Tanya raised their hands.

'I can't donate. I have a health problem,' submitted Bhaskaran.

'Follow me, all the rest of you,' commanded Raghu and walked out of the room in a rush.

As the last of the girls left, Santosh looked at the remaining three people and said, 'Som, you help Tanya with the fashion week. Bhaskaran, you come with me to K Corp. They are planning a press conference and will need advice on journalists' names. I want you to take notes and get Raghu to talk to his friends once he is normal.'

Bhaskaran chuckled but followed Santosh out.

Som was surprised at the sudden turn of events. 'Is it always like this here?' he asked Tanya.

'I guess so,' she replied in a morose tone.

'Will you come with me to the X-tinction office?' she pleaded. 'We have to collect the creatives and other soft copies before we leave for Mumbai tonight.'

'Sure, why not?' said Som. 'I am happy to be of any help except that I don't have a ride. Not yet.'

Tanya smiled a bit. 'Don't worry,' she said.

AROUND TWELVE, Som and Tanya started for the X-tinction office. They stopped a passing three-wheeler and hired it for Nehru Place.

Som was sitting right at the edge of the seat, careful not to brush against Tanya. He bent forward and was looking outside when the auto hit a speed breaker in top gear.

'Uff, ma!' cried Som in pain as his head hit the rickety iron frame on top.

'You can be comfortable. I am fine,' said Tanya as she moved to her right to make more space.

'Thanks,' said Som. 'Where were you before this?'

'I just completed my graduation in Literature from Ferguson College, Pune. My father was in the Army,' she said.

'I see. So, is he now retired?'

'No. He died in the Kargil war in 1999. There was heavy enemy shelling on our army camps in Drass. Papa and a jawan came in the line of fire. In his final moments, Papa had wished he'd rather died on the top of Tiger Hill than be killed by a stray bullet.'

'I am so sorry,' said Som.

'Don't be sorry, please. Colonel Sachdev died for the country, after all,' said Tanya.

Som had now begun to understand the perpetual downcast expression on Tanya's face. *Maybe she still misses her father*, he thought.

After half an hour, they were in the office of Girish Raheja, the marketing head of X-tinction. 'Tanya, come in,' said the fat, balding man. 'And who is he you've got with you today?'

After pleasantries and two cups of coffee, Tanya started packing the CDs and negatives in her bag. Just then, Som got a call from Santosh asking him to join at the K Corp Office in Okhla.

Girish volunteered to drop Tanya back to her Vasant Kunj home on his way to Gurgaon.

'I am going home anyways. I have to catch that Mumbai flight too,' he insisted. Tanya tried hard to refuse but could not think of a good idea.

Som took Tanya's leave. For the first time, she smiled at him.

THE CHAIRMAN'S OFFICE at K Corp headquarters overlooked the railway tracks near Okhla railway station. There were many huge trees surrounding the compound and monkeys seemed to thrive in the thick foliage.

Company Secretary Ganesan and CFO Patwardhan were engaged in some serious deliberations with CMD Rattan Kathuria. In a far corner sat Santosh Yadav, Bhaskaran, and Som.

'Come here, Santosh,' signalled Patwardhan.

'Finally,' Santosh sighed.

'Sit down, gentlemen. I am very happy with your work. Tell Saklani that he will get a bonus if his agency continues to deliver such performance,' said Kathuria.

'Thank you very much, Sir.' Santosh was over the moon.

'What is your name,' asked Kathuria, pointing towards Som. 'You were the one at Rishikesh on Sunday, right?'

'Som ... Somashish Mukherjee, Sir,' introduced Santosh.

'Oh yes,' said Kathuria. 'Good boy, well done. Now listen to what we want to do. Patwardhan, please brief them.'

The CFO took a deep breath and started narrating the plans. 'This year, the revenues from our IT software and hardware businesses will exceed five hundred crore and net profit will be fifty crore. However, we want to aim higher up the value chain and focus on becoming a KPO firm. It means expanding into more cities, hiring more people, and buying more space and equipment. Basically, our expansion plans need an investment of two hundred crore in the next two years if we are to triple our revenues and double our margins.'

Patwardhan paused. 'Are you with me?'

Santosh and Som nodded in unison. Bhaskaran was busy scribbling notes.

'So, we need the money now. This is not an amount that a bank would lend to us, not on the basis of the current turnover. And we are not so well-known yet that we can successfully launch an IPO. It will remain under-subscribed. Are you with me?'

'Sure, Sir,' said Som.

'Therefore, the best route is to approach private equity firms who will buy stake in our company for an attractive amount. They may not get us the full money, but this deal will give us a good valuation and inspire confidence in the public to apply for our shares when we open the IPO.'

'Right, so you are approaching PE firms for stake sale. How much will you offload?' asked Santosh.

'I am ready to sell forty-nine per cent, but will they have appetite to buy that much in an unknown entity?' laughed Kathuria. 'Even if I raise a hundred crore through them, my job is done.'

'How do we support you?' asked Som. Ganesan explained, 'Next month, we will travel to Europe on a roadshow to meet some top PE firms in Geneva and London. Your agency has to help us put together an impressive presentation pack with key facts and figures and support it with employee video films, customer testimonials, and positive media clips. One of you will come to Europe to support us as our corporate communications head. We will organise the appointment letter, visiting card, visa, and all those things. You need not worry, please.'

Som looked at Santosh.

'I'm not sure who will go, but this is a lot of work and I will have to discuss this with Ashish since financial PR is not in our current scope of work,' remarked Santosh.

'Don't worry. I will speak to Saklani,' assured Kathuria. 'You start the work from tomorrow and sit here with Patwardhan.' There was a sense of urgency and finality in his voice.

'And what happens to the press conference?' asked Santosh.

'That will be upon our victorious return,' smiled Patwardhan.

A loud ring interrupted the conversation.

Santosh pulled out his cellphone from his shirt pocket. 'Yes Girish, how are you?'

The voice at the other end was not pleasant. Someone was really agitated and although it was difficult to follow the phrases, the abuses came through loud and clear.

Santosh tried his best to calm the caller down, but eventually gave up. He disconnected the call and rose from the seat. 'You will have to excuse me, Sir. There is a crisis,' he said to Kathuria. 'I will report back tomorrow morning. Thank you.'

Som and Bhaskaran looked apologetically at the K Corp anagement, hesitated and then ran after Santosh.

In the lobby, Santosh told Bhaskaran, 'You are going to Mumbai tonight with Ejaz. I will manage Raghu. Give your notes to Som and pack your bags.'

Santosh was furiously dialling a number on his phone as Bhaskaran gently passed on a paper to Som. 'What is this?' Som asked in a hushed voice as he saw a caricature of Kathuria as a bull on rampage.

Santosh's call had finally connected. He almost screamed into the phone.

'Tanya, this is Santosh here. Why the bloody hell did you slap Girish Raheja?'

Chapter 9

Fly by Night

Ashish Saklani was not happy.

'I had a chat with Girish Raheja last night and he agreed not to report this episode to the MD of X-tinction. He also assured me that the agency would not be penalised for the actions of one stupid individual,' he said.

'Tanya is being taken off the account with immediate effect and I'll see what to do with her now.'

Dr Vibhas Pandey protested. 'She had no choice, Ashish. Instead of dropping her off at Vasant Kunj, he was driving her deep into Mehrauli forest.'

'That was to pick up cloth samples from Remo's studio. Girish wanted Tanya to take them for the press kit,' explained Santosh.

'Why could Girish or Remo not carry them along? Why did Girish not stop when Tanya said she would not like to go there?' countered Dr Pandey.

'Tanya is always like that,' Santosh brushed aside the argument. 'Girish has complained in the past that she does not answer his calls after five p.m., however urgent, and it is always Ejaz who then does the work.'

'But why does Girish call her after five? Ejaz is the account head anyways,' Dr Pandey did not relent.

Ashish Saklani intervened. 'Let's not fight over a silly, insecure, depressed girl here. Vibhas, send her the salary cheque and termination letter. Som and Payal can go to her house and also collect the cellphone and laptop.'

'This is not fair, captain,' objected Dr Pandey.

'Vibhas,' said Ashish, half-closing his toad-like eyes. 'Thinking Caps exists to serve clients and meet their requirements every minute of the day. There is no room for prudish righteousness or irrational behaviour here. We need mature people to run the business.'

'I was a general manager at a five star hotel twenty years ago,' Ashish continued. 'Do you know what kind of harassment the hotel hostesses had to undergo at that point of time? But the girls defied perceptions and broke out of the stereotype image that society had cast them in. It is the same for the PR industry now. You will become what you choose to become.'

Ashish and Santosh then hurried out of Dr Pandey's room and the office.

Ashish told Santosh, 'Put Payal in place of Tanya. And get Bhaskaran to help in the FMCG team. He is not of much use in the media team as Raghu says.'

Som overheard this conversation from his seat in the hall. There was only Dr Pandey and Payal in the office. Ejaz and Bhaskaran were in Mumbai, Raghu Pillai's team was out on media rounds, and Prem Rawat had left for Nainital after his father's sudden demise.

Som's phone buzzed loudly, breaking the silence in the office.

'Bhaskaran,' shouted Som in excitement. 'How is Mumbai?'

'I don't know. I am in Lonavla.'

'What? Isn't your fashion show starting tomorrow? Have you invited the press, handed over the kits?' Som was surprised.

'Ejaz is working on that. I believe in reverse delegation. I told him I was sick and sneaked out of the hotel.'

Som was outraged, but toned down his voice and whispered, 'Why are you playing with your job? You've been acting really funny in office. Every time I see you, there's this grin on your face. What are you upto? Ashish Saklani will do to you what he's done to Tanya.'

'Do you think I care for Saklani's peanuts or what this idiot Raghu teaches me? Once an entrepreneur, always an entrepreneur. I will soon have my own PR agency, *Babumoshai*. Just you wait. You'll be in for a shock!'

It's so typical of Bhaskaran. I should stay miles away from any of his plans now, Som thought.

He was concerned about the way things were going at Thinking Caps. Only last night he had assured ma and baba that he had found a good career path and will even travel abroad to Europe. He could do without shocks in his life now.

'Hero, shall we go now?' Payal Mehra was all dressed up and made up.

Som did not find the endearment flattering. He was anything but a hero.

'Sure, if you're ready,' he said. 'I'm always ready for handsome men,' laughed Payal. And then she went on laughing hysterically as Som blushed all over.

THEY HIRED A taxi to the Vasant Kunj flat where Tanya lived at the ground floor. A servant answered the door. As soon as they entered, a regiment of dogs surrounded them, barking like mad. Som froze where he stood. A German Shepherd was sniffing around his groin and a golden retriever was licking his right hand, wagging her tail joyously.

'Betty, Veronica, Archie, Jaggu ... leave them alone,' commanded a tall, fair lady.

'Hello aunty,' said Payal, as she sprang forward to embrace the mistress of the house.

A couple of hugs and kisses later, Payal pleaded. 'I am suddenly down. Can I borrow a pad, aunty?'

Som pretended not to listen. The dogs had retreated by some feet but continued to maintain a tight vigil on him.

'Oh sorry, this is Som. He joined us a week ago,' Payal introduced. 'Som, this is Tanya's mom.'

'Hello Beta,' said Mrs Sachdev. 'How are you? Please be comfortable. We'll just be back.'

Som liked the way the lady smiled. Her face was pink and full. The expression of contentment on it was so much like his own mother's.

All the dogs, except one, followed the ladies to the bedroom. The German Shepherd sat down near Som's feet with its jaws resting on its paws. Som dared not move a finger.

The house was tastefully decorated and full of trophies and rifles. A photo of the late Colonel was kept on the side table. 'Handsome man!' Som thought.

A maid brought in a tray of soft drinks and biscuits. Som looked at the dog and then at the cola. He wanted to drink but was not sure of the reaction it would evoke from his canine guard. So he kept sitting still.

'Jaggu likes you.' Tanya came in running.

Contrary to Som's expectations, she was neither sad nor sobby. In fact, she looked in good spirits. She was without her trademark thick-rimmed spectacles and was wearing a white suit. Her hair was oiled and pleated back neatly. 'Jaggu used to sit like this near my father,' she said, stroking the dog's head fondly.

Som smiled. It was clear to him that Tanya's thoughts always revolved around her late father.

'I am sorry about yesterday. Here's your cheque and letter. We have been told to collect the office phone and laptop,' said Som regretfully.

'Don't be sorry, Som,' said Tania. 'We should not be sorry for anything. I am not for whatever I have done. That swine had to be taught a lesson. And if the agency wants to work with such people, I don't want to work with the agency.'

'So, what will you do now?' asked Som.

'I have some plans. I'll let you know very soon,' said Tanya.

'Hey, Tanya, don't keep him in suspense. He's interested, can't you see?' taunted Payal. She was back.

All of them laughed at Som's expense. For the first time ever, Som saw Tanya laugh.

'I'll make you hot cheese pakoras,' said Mrs Sachdev. 'Looks like the monsoons are here, finally.'

Tanya got up to draw open the curtains. She then flung open the windows to let fresh breeze come inside the room. As little drops of water fell on her face from the grey sky, she smiled to herself.

All of them chatted for an hour or so and then, when the rain stopped, Payal demanded, 'Now drop me home, hero.' Payal lived in Preet Vihar, not far from Kenny and Som's apartment in Patparganj. So it was logical that they took one taxi.

On the way, at about six p.m., Payal got a call from an unknown number.

'Hi Payal, this is Girish Raheja. I got to know you will now service me. Actually, I didn't fly to Mumbai last night. I'm leaving tonight. I'm just wondering if you'd like to join me as well. Tickets are not a problem. We'll stay at the Taj.'

Payal winked at Som and put the phone on loudspeaker.

She said, 'Hi Girish. I am so happy you called. I am so thrilled that I am actually planning to come over to your house tonight. Your wife will be so very happy to see me. Her sister was my best friend in school!'

'What?' Girish sounded alarmed. 'Shikha never told me about you. Neither did Jyoti.'

'Do you even know which school your sister-in-law went to?' Payal teased.

'Of course. St. Mary's. Both sisters studied there,' he retorted.

'That's right. That makes you my brother-in-law too. So you carry on to Mumbai. I'll give Shikha a nice surprise and then we'll have loads of fun together.'

'Oh, so you're family,' said Girish feebly. 'Great then, we'll sync up once I'm back. Bye.'

Som was amazed at the unabashed skill with which Payal handled a scumbag like Girish. 'Bravo,' he clapped his hands. 'But do you know his wife and her sister?'

'Tanya has seen their photo on his desk. I'll find Shikha Raheja on Facebook,' Payal smiled.

'What if he checks with them first?' asked Som.

'He won't, trust me,' said Payal. 'Won't you come up for a cup of coffee? Come on, I won't do anything to you.'

Som had no reply. Payal cracked up and almost fell off the taxi laughing.

Som shut the door and shouted back, 'Are you always insane, Payal?'

Minutes later, Payal forwarded a text message to Som. It read: *Please don't bring up the Tanya issue with Shikha. It was a misunderstanding. Cheers, Girish.*

DAYS LATER, ON 9 July 2003, Bhaskaran was driving Som to the Indira Gandhi International Airport. 'So, it's settled now, Som. I am moving into your Patparganj apartment with my girlfriend next week.'

'Absolutely not, you may come in alone but only if you pay half the rent,' clarified Som.

'Fine, but listen to me carefully,' said Bhaskaran. 'I am launching my PR agency with a dinner party at Radisson next Saturday. You will come there straight from the airport. OK? See you!'

Som alighted outside Gate No 2 of the international departure terminal. His head was spinning. He didn't know how Bhaskaran got the money and resources to launch his own PR agency. And the party at Radisson sounded really expensive. 'Weird guy!' he thought. 'Why does he want to shift in with me when he has a home in Delhi? Wants to have fun with his girlfriend, maybe.'

The police constable on duty checked Som's passport and air ticket. He examined the Visa carefully, and asked, 'First time going abroad? Wait for twenty minutes. You cannot get inside before three hours of departure.'

So Som pulled his sole luggage – a suitcase – aside and stood watching scores of people who had come to see off their relatives.

There was a busload of folks who had come with someone. One of them held aloft a placard that read 'All the best to Vicky te Soni'. Two men were beating the life out of bhangra drums. Old men and women were seen repeatedly hugging and blessing a man and his newly wed wife. Som looked at the man closely. It was a dark, unshaven face with long, back-brushed hair. A diamond twinkled in the man's right ear.

Som at once recognised the fellow as the guy who had tried to molest Aparna at Vasant Vihar crossing the previous year. His demure wife was wearing cream and red bangles right upto the elbow, and seemed happy and oblivious to her illustrious husband's misadventures. As the duo entered the terminal gate, half-a-dozen women broke down. The group did not budge from its place until the police asked them to clear off. Vicky and Soni bid farewell one last time and then the drums fell silent.

Som was finally let inside by the police constable. After the luggage X-ray, he proceeded to the airline desk. There was a huge queue at the Air France counter. Men, women, and children of all ages and sizes had lined up for the flight to Paris. Som noted that Vicky was in front of him in the line.

The lady at the counter announced, 'Only twenty kilos per head, please.' Soon, suitcases opened up left, right and centre. The smell of aloo paranthas and pickles filled the air. Packets of Maggi, chips, and apple juice were being thrown around. Some people ran back to the entry gate, trying to hand over stuff to their waiting relatives. The police, however, did not permit the transfer of goods.

Vicky did not have excess baggage. He told the airline agent, 'Going to London by Paris.'

'Connecting flight?' the girl asked. 'Yes ji,' Vicky nodded.

At the immigration desk, the official asked Som, 'Your passport was issued in 1996 but you are travelling only now. Why?'

'Did not get Visa, Sir,' Som regretted. 'I had applied for a British Visa under the school exchange prgramme.'

In the waiting lounge, foreigners and business travellers had chosen to sit on one side while families and tour groups were seated on the other. The family area was full of activity even at midnight. Children were chasing each other across rows and falling on luggage pieces. Some women were breastfeeding infants and some men were joining sofas to prepare a bed.

Som sat down near a group of Caucasians. Two ladies were talking excitedly and exchanging photographs. 'Look here,' said the red-haired lady, 'cows in the middle of Connaught Place. What a sight!'

'Look at mine,' responded the blonde, 'this family of beggars lives under a tree near a garbage dump in Noida. This man is the patriarch. He found a wife and produced kids right under the tree. How unbelievable! I gave them old shoes and a pair of jeans. God bless them!'

With such generous donors, who needs the International Monetary Fund, Som wondered.

The aircraft was huge. It could carry over three hundred people easily and had plenty of room. But a group of passengers had blocked the aisle, debating on the best corner for their luggage.

So the boarding line got stuck and did not move for the next ten minutes, until the flight purser intervened.

Among the last to board the plane was a group of MBA students from Indian Institute of Business Management. They were all wearing branded T-shirts. The private institute regularly advertised its free Europe tours in newspapers to attract students. It was quite another matter that the cost was recovered through the hefty fees.

As soon as the plane took off, the students roared out aloud. Some even whistled. It seemed they were on a roller-coaster ride. Som found the uncivilised screaming most despicable. But the students were upbeat – teasing each other, mimicking animal voices and making catcalls. 'Oh Juhi, why don't you shut up?' asked a boy loudly. 'I can do whatever I feel like. This is not Barabanki, we are going to Paris!' the girl shouted back.

It occurred to Som that most of these aspiring MBAs were from small towns and had not even boarded a domestic flight, let alone travel abroad. 'Like me, they too migrate to bigger cities in search of careers and are willing to even sell ancestral property to pay for their higher education,' he mused.

Seated next to Som was the mother of a London cabbie. She knew no tongue other than Punjabi and was not even literate. So when the air hostess asked her if she would like a vegetarian meal, she asked Som, '*Kudi kee dusdi hai?*'

The eight-hour-long flight was uneventful but tiring. Not able to sleep, Som played an unwilling translator and even filled up some declaration forms for his co-passenger. When they got off at Charles De Gaulle airport where Som had to take a connecting flight to Geneva, the lady caught hold of his arm. '*Rab twauda bhala kare puttar.*'

It was a long time since anybody had blessed Som. He felt a surge of emotions overpower him. But he kept walking slowly towards Terminal 2F. And then he saw something that surprised him.

Vicky was moving swiftly towards the exit door with just a small bag in hand. And before Som's eyes, he boarded a taxi and disappeared. His wife, Soni, was moving around in the terminal with a trolley, searching for her lost husband. Recognising Som as a fellow-passenger, she came upto him for help. 'My husband is missing. Can I make a phone call, please?' she asked him.

Vicky's phone was unreachable. After a few more unsuccessful attempts, Soni gave up and sat down crying.

Som looked at his phone. There were three new messages.

The first SMS read: *We wish you a very happy 22nd birthday. Ma, Baba, and Rahul.*

The second read: *Have a nice flight, Som. Goodnight. Tanya.*

The third read: *Kathuria arrested in Delhi for fraud. Please come back by next flight. Use credit card. Santosh.*

Chapter 10

Love and Loss

It was now September 2004.

Fourteen months had passed since that fateful night when Som had to fly back to Delhi without seeing an inch of Europe.

As promised, Bhaskaran had indeed launched his own PR firm. He had named it 'Testosterone', much to the chagrin of friends and foes alike. A small fortune had gone into funding the agency. Bhaskaran's parents had sold off their house in Mayur Vihar for their son's business and had moved to Chennai.

Dr Vibhas Pandey, who was generally upset with Saklani's arbitrary methods and high-handedness, and enraged at Tanya's unfair dismissal, had gladly accepted Bhaskaran's offer to head operations for Testosterone. Payal and Tanya came on board almost immediately. Som had to be coaxed, cajoled, and brainwashed to fall in line. He was the last one to join.

In effect, Bhaskaran had erected his business on the grave of Thinking Caps. With just Santosh Yadav and Ejaz left to deliver service, Saklani lost one client after the other until he finally shut shop.

All the marketing and business development for Testosterone was done by Bhaskaran himself. He owned seventy per cent of the agency and gifted the remaining thirty per cent to Dr Pandey. Som refused any stock options and had instead settled for an annual CTC of eight lakh.

This made him a superstar back home in Kolkata. At first, Ram and Savita could not believe their ears, but slowly realised that Som had indeed made it big in Delhi. Every month, Som would courier a cheque to his father, and Ram Mukherjee would stand by the pond, trying to remember Som's face as he had last seen him over two years ago.

The launch of Testosterone and the sheer volume of work that the core team of Som, Tanya, and Payal had to execute meant that Som could not go home for Durga Puja the previous year. But he was hoping to go back this year, before Vijaya Dashami in October.

The mystery around Bhaskaran's girlfriend had cleared. It was Payal whom he had fallen for. Of course, that did not prevent her from flirting with Som every now and then. And each time Som complained to Bhaskaran, the latter just laughed the matter off.

'I simply don't understand,' Som had once told Tanya. 'What kind of man can tolerate his girlfriend making passes at someone else?'

Tanya had said, 'If that someone else happens to be you, the man can forever rest in peace.'

Som did not get it.

The agency now had eleven project-based clients and three on monthly retainership. The project clients doled out good money running into lakhs for a single event. These were big, high-profile events like fashion shows, movie premieres, celebrity visits, and even royalty weddings. The organisers were never short of money but the work lasted from two to four months and usually peaked in winter. But Bhaskaran was not very happy with his business mix. He wanted the percentage of assured recurring monthly revenue to go up to half of his total earnings.

Meanwhile, the team criss-crossed the country, working simultaneously on all assignments with some task-based help from local freelance PR professionals. Dr Pandey looked after vendor management and coordination, infrastructure, documentation, invoicing, and HR. He also hired a graduate from YMCA as Admin Assistant.

Testosterone was located in Okhla, not very far from the K Corp office that the police had sealed after nabbing the management. There were tales abound about how Ganesan set fire to the office to evade arrest, and was burnt to death. Som always had an eerie feeling while driving past the building.

But today he was not alone. Tanya was with him in the car and they had a long drive to Jaipur ahead.

'Mummy, I'll be fine. Don't worry. Som is with me.' Tanya assured Mrs Sachvev on the phone.

'That's a wrong assurance to give your mother,' warned Som. 'I am driving to Jaipur for the first time and you know I'm a new driver.'

Tanya smiled. She was wearing a deep red shirt and blue jeans. Tired after a long day at work, she removed her shoes and folded a leg. Taking off her spectacles, she asked, 'What keeps you going, Som? Aren't you tired? We could have taken the morning Shatabdi.'

'I don't know what keeps me going, Tanya. What I do know is that I had made a promise to myself two years ago. I wanted to have a meaningful career, establish myself, and become somebody. Yes, I'm doing alright but I don't feel settled yet and the fear of falling down again keeps me on my toes,' Som explained.

'How would you fall down again? Financially? Is money your sole benchmark?' Tanya probed. 'Or do you think you will fall in character and thought and lose your ideals?'

'Oh no!' Som shot back. 'I will never compromise on my ideals for anything. It's just that it's so hard to find work that one can enjoy and also make money out of. It seems too good to last forever.'

'Yes, too good to last forever,' Tanya repeated.

'And what about the settling down part?' she asked nervously. 'Hasn't your mom selected a Bengali girl for you yet?'

'I am sure she has,' Som's eyes lit up as he remembered his mother. 'But I haven't for sure. I don't think I'm ready for such commitments yet.'

'Not all relationships demand commitment,' Tanya continued. 'Being close to someone can bring a lot of happiness and peace. Why do you see bondage there?'

'Tell me about it,' Som laughed sarcastically. 'Haven't I seen Bhaskaran go broke every month buying gifts for Payal?'

'Not all girls are the same,' Tanya protested. 'There are those who are willing to break any barriers for love.'

'Maybe, but it ultimately boils down to the question of financial stability and a good career. Trust me.'

'Som, you're trivialising the whole thing. You are talking just like a Punjabi.'

'And you're talking like a perfect Bengali, Tanya. To sleep on a broken bed and dream of utopia! All rubbish ... Plain excuse for inertia.'

Both of them kept quiet for a minute. Was this argument going too far?

Then Som commented jovially, 'By the way, my ma thinks that Punjabi women are as aggressive as their menfolk, waiting to gobble up innocents like me in Delhi.'

'Tell me about it,' Tanya was amused. 'Bengali mothers-in-law are the most ferocious in the world. They don't yield a finger's space to their daughters-in-law.'

They laughed out loud together.

As evening passed into night, the traffic on the Delhi-Jaipur highway grew thinner. As the car was about to cross Gurgaon, Som switched on the radio. A popular channel was playing golden oldies.

It was Kishore Kumar singing an evergreen number from the film *Khaamoshi*. '*Woh shaam kucch ajeeb thi, yeh shaam bhi kucch ajeeb hai* ...'

Indeed, for some reason, it seemed to Tanya that she and Som were together for ages now.

Tanya's heart was in turmoil. It burnt with love and longing, while Som moved on from one topic to another, totally impervious to her feelings. He had no time for love, it seemed.

Or how else could he not understand her feelings for him? She had been like his shadow all these months, taking care of his needs to the last detail as he delivered PR coverage for one client after the other. Not once had he paused to think why she agreed to accompany him on a long drive when she could have taken the train to Jaipur. 'Stupid boy!' Tanya smiled to herself as she imagined how Som would look dressed as a Bengali groom, perched precariously on a white horse. She bit her finger to muffle a small chuckle and then closed her eyes.

Oblivious to Tanya's fantasy about their marriage, Som whistled and cooed as he drove the car until the radio programme came to an end.

He looked at Tanya who was now fast asleep, completely lost in her romantic dreams. He carefully used his left hand to remove the spectacles from over Tanya's eyes and then placed it in the glove box.

He decided to drive faster, now that they were well past Manesar and nearing Neemrana village. The full moon gave company to his thoughts as his mind wandered back to Kolkata, his home, college, and Chandni.

Som did not know why he still remembered Chandni or of what use those memories were. If anything, they acutely reminded him of his mundane insignificance, of his gross inadequacies as compared to the IITian Ashok Kumar. Whatever Som did, Ashok still seemed taller in stature. And hence, Som was still not satisfied with himself.

It was half past ten when Som drove through the gates of Rambagh Palace Hotel in Jaipur. The sprawling palace was a former royal residence and a symbol of grandeur.

Som was simply awed by the architecture and environs that surrounded him. Tanya was bleary-eyed but happy to be garlanded and greeted in traditional Rajasthani style by the hotel staff. She looked beautiful with the *tikka* on her forehead.

The dinner buffet was laid out on a terrace near the gardens at the rear of the hotel. There were fire-eaters and folk dancers to entertain the numerous Indian and foreign guests. An expert was also tying pink turbans for whoever fancied the headgear.

Som was thrilled. The ambience seemed to instantly wipe away all fatigue from the long drive. Tanya excused herself to freshen up.

Som walked across to a corner of the terrace and looked up at the domes and *chatris* on higher floors. 'Magnificent!' he thought as he beheld the intricate filigree work on the railings.

And then, walking backwards, Som collided against something.

A bone china dinner plate crashed onto the marble floor with a crackling sound.

All guests, entertainers, and waiters stopped in their activities to look at the site of accident.

Som stood still, totally aghast at the damage he had done. He had ruined the dinner and clothes of a lady guest. As she wiped off stains of food from her saree, the lady looked angrily at the offender. Then the anger turned into a pleasant surprise.

'Som, is that you?' asked Chandni Roy.

Som was stupefied. His world went into a tailspin. His heart skipped several beats. He could not stop gaping at his first crush as she stood before him in flesh and blood.

Tanya rushed towards Som but stopped a few feet away as she heard him speak.

'Chandni, I didn't think we would ever meet again.'

THE AGONY OF love is more intense than hellfire, they say. Tanya had a first-hand experience of this condition that night. She was in deep anguish and felt utterly bereft of all peace. The way Som looked at Chandni killed every dream in her eyes. As she tossed and turned around restlessly in the bed, she felt a sharp knife cutting slowly through her chest.

In the morning when Som came knocking, Tanya opened the door without looking at him.

Som got worried seeing her so downcast and with swollen eyes.

'What's the matter, haven't you slept?' asked Som.

'I am not feeling well,' Tanya replied. She walked to her bed and got into the sheets. 'You carry on today. I'll rest here.'

Som was puzzled but did not probe further. He called the room service for some light breakfast for Tanya and requested the receptionist for medicine. He sat there by the bedside until Tanya had finished her chocolate drink. And then he bid her goodbye.

'Who is Chandni, Som? You never mentioned her before,' said Tanya, masking her curiosity.

'She was a classmate in college in Kolkata,' explained Som. 'I was shocked to see her here. Guess what, she's a visiting faculty at the Jaipur Nritya Academy we are inaugurating today. They'll open up a branch in Kolkata soon.'

Som wanted to say something else but stopped abruptly.

His words offered little solace to Tanya. She was careful to note the visible excitement in Som's voice as he spoke about Chandni.

Later that morning, Tanya called Mrs Sachdev.

'Mummy, can you send Bahadur with the car to pick me up? I am not feeling well and Som has to stay here for two more nights.'

On the way to the inauguration event, Som and Chandni got to talk a little more than they had the previous night after the food mishap.

Actually, when they met this morning for breakfast, it was Chandni who had suggested that they travel in the same car to the venue. What Som had not known then was that Tanya would be suddenly indisposed.

As the Mercedes passed by the broad road outside the state legislative assembly, Chandni said, 'I am happy that you're doing well, Som. It's really odd how we meet after two years like this. The last I heard from Garima was that you were studying at IIMC.'

Som smiled. It was flattering to know that Chandni had kept track of him and cared for him in some way. He, on the other hand, had not ever asked Basu about her. 'Yes, it's been a roller-coaster ride,' Som said. 'I'm not yet where I want to be but I'm fine, I guess. What about you? How is Ashok?'

Chandni kept quiet and looked outside the car window.

Turning her head back and looking straight into Som's eyes, she said, 'I am not yet married.'

Som stared at Chandni's face now. He had never seen her from such close quarters. The sun shone on her fair skin, revealing some blemishes here and there. She was still very beautiful, but it was evident that she had not been taking good care of herself.

'Those who do not value love, do not get love,' said Chandni. 'And I'm so sorry that I was rude to you when you met me at the Victoria Memorial.'

She placed her palm on Som's left fist.

'Oh please, Chandni, do not embarrass me,' Som exclaimed. 'How were you supposed to react otherwise? Imagine me springing up on you like that in the final days of college. Besides, you were already engaged, weren't you?'

'Yes I was,' she said. 'Ashok and I were to marry in the winter of 2003, a year ago. Although the marriage had been arranged by my father, in my heart, I had come to accept him as my husband.

But he never turned up for the marriage, he never came back from the US. They say he lives with a Brazilian girl in Florida. The irony is that I have never even met him, only spoken to him once on phone.'

She broke down.

Som felt terribly sorry. He did not know what to say. He had never thought it would turn out to be like this for Chandni. All along, he had thought of only himself as a loser.

Suddenly, Som felt no competition with Ashok. He could not relate to the man any more. He was happy to be where he was and doing whatever he did.

'I should tell Tanya this story,' he thought.

In the meanwhile, Chandni wiped off her tears.

'So, tell me what you do,' she said to Som.

'Well, I am a public relations professional,' said Som. 'I travel all over India arranging press conferences and product launches. Sometimes, I also do serious stuff like shareholder meetings, IPOs, and writing white papers.'

'Wow, sounds interesting. But what is a white paper?' Chandni asked. 'I have seen a lot of pink papers in college, as you would know!' she laughed.

Som grinned. Of course, he too had once bought a perfumed letterpad on Valentine's Day for Chandni. But it was another matter that he could not finalise the love letter.

'A white paper is like a research paper on some topic of public interest,' Som explained. 'It helps companies and organisations explain current issues to media and laymen, and build opinion in favour of their activities.'

'So, you're a spin doctor?' asked Chandni. 'Isn't there a lot of money involved in getting good coverage? Bribes and gifts, I mean?' She was inquisitive.

'Oh, please don't use that term,' implored Som. 'It sounds really shady. We do promote our clients in society but do not twist and misrepresent facts. We do bank on relationships but never pay bribes or give expensive gifts like some small-time players,' he explained. 'And yes, there are many other PR tools and methods which I did not mention to you,' he added.

'I didn't mean offence, Som,' clarified Chandni. 'It's a new field ... what you are doing. I think it's cool!'

THAT EVENING, AS Som and Chandni returned from the dance academy launch, they met Tanya at the staircase near the hotel reception.

'Where are you going, Tanya?' Som was bewildered.

'I'm leaving for Delhi, Som. Mummy has sent Bahadur,' she said. Tanya's face was still swollen and red.

'Chandni, this is Tanya,' Som introduced the ladies to each other.

Chandni looked fondly at Tanya, observing her carefully.

Tanya quickly scanned Chandni from top to toe. 'So, this is what Som likes,' she thought. 'Maybe I don't measure up to his Bengali tastes.'

'I like your kurti very much. You look really beautiful in it,' Chandni complimented Tanya.

Tanya managed to stretch her lips.

As she stepped into the car, Bahadur closed the door. Recognising Som, he whispered to him, *'Madamji bahut boli, aaj mat aao. Som Babu ke saath aao. Par yeh kahan mani?'*

Som did not understand why Tanya insisted on leaving against her mother's wishes.

After the car was gone, she asked, 'Som, is Tanya your girlfriend?'

Som was taken aback at the question. 'No, I mean, yes we are friends and she is a girl. Yes. But not in that way.' He spoke like an ass and knew it immediately.

Chandni smiled.

On the highway to Delhi, Tanya's car was zipping through a maze of trucks. 'Drive faster, Bahadur. What's the matter with you?' Tanya scoffed.

Women and their strange ways! Bahadur grimaced. *She must have fought with Som Babu. First driving two hundred kilometers in the night only to return the very next day. What sane person would behave like this?*

Tanya had finalised her plans.

She would resign from Testosterone and go back to Pune to her cousins' house. She would try to forget Som and never again return to Delhi.

Part Two

Chapter 11

Homecoming

Bahadur heaved a sigh of relief as the car rolled into Vasant Kunj. Mrs Sachdev came out of the house in an instant.

'*Ki hoya, puttar*?' she asked.

Tanya flung herself into her mummy's arms. The four dogs hovered around them, wagging their tales in solidarity.

As Tanya went on crying ceaselessly, her mother realised that there was some serious reason behind it. How she wished Colonel Sachdev was alive to comfort his baby!

Bahadur wanted to retire for the night with his bottle of rum. He stood dumbfounded watching the two weep as the mother too had started crying now.

In Jaipur, Som was weighing his options. With Tanya back in Delhi, he decided to quickly wrap up things and leave early the very next day.

When he spoke to Bhaskaran about his plans, the latter suggested that Som could proceed to Kolkata for a short personal break since there were not any major activities lined up for a month or so. In fact, Som could fly out from Delhi the next day itself and hand over his car to the office peon at the airport.

Chandni was very happy to know that Som would accompany her in the flight to Kolkata. 'Garima and Basu will be so happy to see you,' she said to Som. The next morning, Chandni joined Som in his car for the long drive back to Delhi.

Som could not believe that he was actually spending so much time with her. They talked like the most intimate of friends, chatting up everything under the sun. It was the first time that Som got to know about Chandni's views and opinions on a wide range of subjects. Their perspectives did not match most of the time, especially on topics of individual choice versus social conventions. Nevertheless, Som respected Chandni's thoughts and did not let the conversation influence their newfound friendship.

'You know, Chandni, whatever may have happened, you have your entire life ahead. You must take care of yourself,' said Som.

Chandni became a little conscious but smiled, and said, 'I will.'

When the aircraft landed at the Kolkata airport, Chandni's parents and elder brother, Partho, were surprised to see her walk out with Som in tow. However, it was a pleasant surprise.

Biswajeet Roy doted on his daughter. Since that fateful day the previous year when Ashok had not boarded the flight to India, he had seen Chandni slowly wilt away. But today, she looked as happy as a lark, chatting with Som as she waved out her hand.

Chandni's mother, Kalyani, and brother stood wondering who this lanky fellow was. 'He looks Bengali all right, doesn't he, *Khokon*?' Kalyani asked her son.

Som did not expect to meet Chandni's family at the airport. He was totally unprepared for the close scrutiny that he was subsequently subjected to. 'Come with us in the car, Khokon will drop you to Behala. He is anyways going that way,' insisted Biswajeet.

Meanwhile, Savita had not slept one wink that afternoon. She wasn't expecting Som to come before October, but when he called to announce that he was on his way, she almost had a heart seizure. With Rahul in college and her husband in office, Savita had got enough time to prepare a banquet of sorts. On the menu were Som's favourite boneless Pabda fish curry, banana stem vegetable, lamb in thick gravy, and tomato chutney. A bowl of sweet curd and rasogollas had been diligently ordered from Gopal's sweet shop.

Meanwhile, at Chandni's home, Som was treated to a wide variety of snacks and foods – deep-fried cutlets of fish, egg, and chicken, and blueberry cheese cake from the most popular bakery in Park Street. Chandni looked on smiling as Som tried a few of the items. Her mother was frantically issuing instructions to the maidservant, ensuring that Som had his belly full.

Chandni's teenage sister was prancing around in tight shorts with an iPod hanging from her neck. She barely acknowledged Som.

How different Chandni seems from her sister, Som thought. He had never imagined that he'd be sitting in the Roy home and feasting, not even at the peak of his obsession with Chandni. And here he was, doing exactly that. He did not understand why he was being meted out such special treatment. Or were the Roys always so hospitable?

On the pretext of fetching water, Kalyani called Chandni to another room. 'How much does he earn?' she asked. Chandni was surprised. 'I don't know and I don't care, Ma. He's a classmate whom I last met over two years ago,' Chandni said.

'Classmate my foot,' Kalyani said. 'Didn't I see the way you were laughing with him, all your thirty-two teeth flashing?'

'Ma,' Chandni tried to protest but Kalyani did not listen. 'I told your father to go with khokon to his house. Let's check out his folks. Even if they are half-decent, we will explore the matter further,' she said.

'But Ma, we are not in a relationship. We are just getting to know each other. Som is a nice boy but this is like forcing me on him. This is not the time to think of our marriage,' Chandni pleaded.

Kalyani snapped back, 'Then when will the right time come? When he's done everything with you? I can't have you waste time sampling boys like this. Your broken marriage has already marred Pinky's prospects.'

Tears welled up in Chandni's eyes as she ran to her room.

In the living room, Som had finished the last morsel of his fish cutlet. Biswajeet and Partho returned from somewhere. 'Come, let's go,' Partho told Som.

The Roys had a thriving garment export business and also owned a supermarket on Diamond Harbour Road near Behala. And though they had no work there at night, they accompanied Som only to assess his eligibility for marriage to Chandni.

Savita's knees trembled as she saw Som's face after two years. Som too could not hold back his tears and rushed forward to touch his mother's feet. Savita embraced her son. A few sobs and cries later, she noticed the two gentlemen standing at the door.

'That's Mr Biswajeet Roy and his son Partho. We met at the airport,' Som introduced.

Savita did not understand but welcomed them nevertheless. Rahul was home and greeted his elder brother warmly. 'Where is my Ninja game?' he whispered. 'Sorry, didn't have time but I'll buy you a Playstation,' said Som. Rahul had never felt happier in life.

Ram Mukherjee could not say much to Som. 'Stay with us for a month at least,' he said in a choked voice.

With slight persuasion, the Roys gladly stayed back for dinner and thoroughly enjoyed the traditional dishes. Som was already feeling full. So he excused himself to refresh and change. Biswajeet Roy got the opportunity he wanted. 'Mr Mukherjee, my daughter, Chandni, talks a lot about Somashish. He's a bright boy. But you see, talent needs nurturing. He can earn crores, not just lakhs.' Glancing around at the house, he continued, 'Send him to America. I will buy him an ad agency there. After all, he's just like Partho to me.'

Ram Mukherjee's jaw dropped at Biswajeet's suggestion. His hand stopped short of his mouth and slowly withdrew back to the dinner plate. Savita was also taken aback completely at the proposal. The Roys were complete strangers, who had met them for the first time and they were already offering to sponsor Som to the US!

'Isn't this the father of the same Chandni who was to get married to an IITian?' Savita thought. 'Why are they so interested in Som now?'

Drawing a sip of water from the steel tumbler, Ram said, 'Biswajeet Babu, I am not entirely aware, at this stage, about Som's relationship with you or your daughter. But thanks for your suggestion. Our family will decide what is best for our son.'

Biswajeet did not like being snubbed thus. 'Well, let me tell you then, Ram Babu, your son and my daughter were classmates in college and, if I am not wrong, they like each other. Now that I have met him, I quite like him and want to help him shape his career so that they can get married. After all, Chandni cannot reside here, can she, Khokon?' he sought Partho's approval.

'No, Baba,' Partho agreed.

'Well, apologies for my ignorance. I will ask my grown-up son about his marriage plans. Maybe he forgot to update me in the hustle and bustle of Delhi's life,' Ram replied, bitterly.

Biswajeet began to say something but Partho interjected. 'Baba, we are getting late,' he said.

The senior Roy looked at Ram and Savita Mukherjee. The hosts looked tense and uncomfortable. Paying heed to Partho's hint, Biswajeet said, 'Of course, yes. I must thank you for your gracious hospitality. *Boudi* cooks really well. And yes, please pardon my impetuousness. I said things that could have waited for another day, maybe. After all, I am the father of a young daughter. I hope you understand.'

Ram managed a feeble smile. He was burning with indignation. *How dare Som put him in such an embarassing situation?*

Som emerged from the bedroom in fresh clothes as the Roys were walking out.

'God bless you, son. See you soon,' Biswajeet patted Som's shoulders as he bid goodbye.

No sooner had the two vanished into the darkness of the narrow alley before the house than Ram called out sternly to Som. 'I want to have a word with you and your ma.'

Som did not know what was going on. Savita looked worried. The two followed Ram back to the living room.

He sat down on a wooden chair and, after drawing in a deep breath, he said, 'Som, I understand that you are a big man now. The twenty-five thousand rupees you send me each month is a testimony to that. Indeed, my heart swells with pride when I talk about you to my colleagues in office. Even my boss regards me highly these days. I was overjoyed to see you today. It was a good surprise. But what an ugly shock have you brought along, Som?

'Who is Biswajeet Roy? Why did he come to my house and shamelessly offer to buy you? Who is his daughter and for how many years has this drama continued now? Why was I not told about this earlier? You think you have grown too big, Som?' Ram's voice was trembling.

With a tone of finality, he said, 'You can do whatever you want and go wherever you wish to. And please take your cheques back. I haven't encashed any of them, as you very well know.'

Som was visibly shaken. He felt terrible, hearing his father's words. He struggled to understand what must have happened to arouse his father's anger so much. 'What happened, Ma?' he asked Savita in a failing voice.

A sad Savita explained, 'Mr Roy wanted to send you to America at his expense so that you and Chandni can get married. Your father and I were unprepared for such talk. After all, you never shared anything about Chandni these last two years, Shona.'

Som shot back immediately, 'That's because there was nothing to share at all. I met Chandni again just two nights ago in Jaipur. And, by coincidence, I got my leave sanctioned now so we boarded the flight to Kolkata together.'

Ram looked at Savita. 'How does Som know this Chandni girl? Ask him,' he said.

'I knew her in college but there was nothing more to it, Baba,' Som replied. 'She was supposed to get married last year. Unfortunately, her marriage didn't happen. I now know why her father and brother insisted on dropping me home today.'

Ram was incredulous. After deep thought, he said in disgust, 'I am not getting into this conversation now. We'll talk tomorrow. But please do not marry this girl, whoever else you may choose to. Otherwise, your life will be ruined.'

'The fault is not with the girl, uncle. It's her family that is pushing her to the edge.'

All of them turned towards the entrance door from where the booming voice originated.

It was Basu. Behind him stood his wife, Garima.

Som and Savita were overjoyed to see the guests. Ram Mukherjee quickly got up. He never quite liked Basu. But Garima should be blessed and received well, he thought.

THE MOOD IN the room was sombre. Garima had just narrated the story of Chandni's great misfortune, explaining how she had slipped into depression after Ashok's no-show at the wedding. Biswajeet and Partho had even travelled to the US to convince Ashok, but he was apparently frolicking on Miami beach with a Brazilian girl.

Soon after, Biswajeet had a cardiac arrest.

'The only wish that now consumes the family, day and night, is Chandni's marriage. While she herself tries to remain occupied with her dance classes, her parents and brother run about scanning every potential groom in town. They are so desperate that they are willing to consider even non-Bengali candidates,' Garima had concluded.

'It is really sad. Som liked that girl but she was already engaged then,' sighed Savita.

'And also, I was a nobody then, Ma,' Som reminded.

'So, what do you think now?' asked Ram. 'The girl should not suffer like this. I don't care if you settle in the US,' he declared as he went to his bedchamber.

Som looked up at the ceiling as all eyes turned towards him.

'I don't know,' he said. 'It is for the first time that I have known her views and ideas, and they are quite different than those of mine. Chandni is very measured and pragmatic, and she believes in social approval. You know how I am. I flow with the wind and can never tolerate her parents' control over our destiny. Yes, she is beautiful and very kind at heart. But can she dream with me?' he asked.

Garima was irritated. 'What gibberish are you saying? It's not making any sense to me.'

Basu intervened. 'Don't force him, please. He is mad, and he wants Chandni to also go mad like him. Only two years ago, he would have died to even touch her feet. Look how he is acting pricey now!'

The argument did not reach any conclusion. Som asked for some time to think over the proposal.

Later that night, he sent a text message to Bhaskaran: *Marriage proposal at twenty-four. American ad agency in dowry. Shall I bite the bait?*

Chapter 12

The Groom

Tanya's phone kept ringing for a long time.

She looked at it but did not take the call. It was Som.

After some moments, she got an SMS. It read: *Hi Tanya, how are you feeling? Have reached Kolkata safely. Will spend a month here. You take care.*

'Of course he will spend a month there. Now that he's got Chandni, what does he care if I live or die?'

And then the phone rang again. It was Payal this time.

'What are you doing here like a fool while Som is in Kolkata?' she demanded.

Tanya did not understand.

'Arre *Kamli*, he's getting married to some Bong babe,' Payal explained. 'You will be left with his articles and photos as memoirs.'

The news did not surprise Tanya in the least. She had been expecting it all along. Only last night, she had a dream about Som and Chandni making out in the hotel lawns. Stricken with grief, Tanya had fainted in the dream.

In the interim, Bhaskaran was busy packing his suitcase. He had to personally go and investigate the strange situation Som had landed in. After all, he could not lose his friend and Client Servicing Director to some freak conspiracy!

Ashish Saklani had risen again like a phoenix and had floated a new PR agency called 'Adrenalin'. Bhaskaran understood from the name that it was meant to counter Testosterone's USP – youth and energy. It was to only protect Som from any possible overtures that Bhaskaran had sent him vacationing to Kolkata, but it seemed that Som had other greater temptations at hand.

With a large business summit to be hosted in Delhi in November, Bhaskaran could do without attrition.

THE NEXT MORNING, Bhaskaran checked into a five star hotel in Kolkata. He sent Som an SMS: *Thought I'd surprise you. Am here at the ITC. Let's meet. New business opportunity.*

A bleary-eyed Som wondered what on earth had got into Bhaskaran. Could the fellow not leave him alone for even two days? And all this drama after egging him on to go on a month's leave!

The two colleagues and friends met in the lobby of the hotel in Shonar Bangla. Som had travelled a long way from Behala in a dirty cab and was visibly irritated.

'What do you think you're doing with my life?' he yelled at Bhaskaran. 'One moment you send me to Kolkata for vacation and the next day you turn up here to completely ruin it!'

'Babumoshai!' said Bhaskaran, grimacing. 'I need money to repay thirty lakh to my parents. How can I say no to money? I know you want to get married but you have to earn money too!'

They quarrelled for long and then Som gave up, exasperated. 'When I get back to Delhi, I will move out of that Patparganj flat. I don't want to live with you any more.'

The new business opportunity walked in with a large briefcase. Inside it were wads of five hundred rupee notes. Mr Aggarwal was the regional sales head of a tractor manufacturing company. The firm wanted to organise a Bollywood night at Benares and invite the biggest farmers in eastern Uttar Pradesh to the show. They had the rabi crop sowing season in mind and wanted top-of-mind recall when the field sales campaigners went to villages.

A cash advance of two lakh was paid to Bhaskaran immediately, and the balance five lakh was to be paid in cheque after the show.

Som could not fathom how Bhaskaran could accept the money without even checking star dates and appointments. 'I can't do it alone. Need Tanya or Payal to help. Managing item girls is not my cup of tea,' Som declared.

Bhaskaran assured Som that Tanya will join him in Benares in a week. And then, he offered Som a salary hike to make it ten lakh per annum. Som bargained hard and they settled for twelve.

'Come, let's have lunch,' offered Bhaskaran. As the two got up from the sofa, Som's cellphone rang out.

It was Basu.

'Chandni wants to meet you, Som. In fact, Garima is also there this afternoon. See if you can go to Tollygunj,' Basu said.

Som took in a deep breath. It seemed that this matter would have to be disposed off one way or the other. Given Chandni's edgy situation, Som would have to take an honest decision. And it would be one of the biggest decisions in his life so far.

Bhaskaran offered to come along if it didn't inconvenience Som. The latter did not mind at all.

Chandni was sitting with Garima on the terrace of her residence. Som and Bhaskaran walked up the stairs, dodging pieces of old wrought iron furniture.

Som introduced Bhaskaran. 'Meet my friend, room-mate and employer. He's the most cunning person I have met in my life,' he said, laughing.

Chandni was amused by the description. 'And yet you seem to love him, Som. How else does he possess your life?' she asked.

Bhaskaran clapped his hands in glee. 'I like your sense of judgement, Ms Roy. You already seem to know me better than Som.'

'I don't know you yet, but I like your pony tail. Do you ever dance?' Chandni asked Bhaskaran.

'You will be most surprised to know that I did the Nataraja dance in school. And they chose me because of my long hair.'

Chandni was in splits. 'Why don't you show us the dance then?' she teased.

Plates of cookies and cups of tea were sent upstairs by Kalyani. After some rounds of casual conversation, Garima told Bhaskaran, 'Come, Mr CEO. Som and Chandni need to have a word together. We will host you downstairs.'

'Of course, by all means,' agreed Bhaskaran, and followed Garima down to the living room where Biswajeet and Kalyani Roy were busy in an animated discussion.

Chandni said to Som, 'You have an interesting friend there.'

'Oh yes,' said Som. 'He's quite a character, believe me!'

Chandni looked at the setting sun and said, 'Do you remember, Som? It was on an evening like this that we had met at the Victoria Memorial. I knew what you wanted to say but I was not in a position then to entertain any thoughts other than those of my marriage to Ashok. I had felt really guilty afterwards, hurting your sentiments like that.'

'No, please. Don't say that,' Som requested.

'Time has come a full circle,' she continued. 'Our chance encounter in Jaipur helped remove a lot of guilt from my mind. I found a new friend in you. But see, where it's gone now. My family has begun to link us up despite my protests. I am extremely sorry for whatever happened at your home last night. But please do not feel pressurised to take any decision.'

Som looked at Chandni and asked, 'What do *you* want?'

Chandni took up a pebble and started drawing lines on the terrace wall.

'Honestly, in such matters, I would rather leave the decision to my parents. That was exactly what I did two years ago. It is only with the collective blessings of all elders that a marriage can be truly successful. You don't marry an individual, you marry a family, after all,' Chandni reflected.

Som was quiet. He could not understand how a beautiful, intelligent, modern woman like Chandni could leave such a critical decision to her parents. And, that too, after a disastrous previous engagement.

He said, 'Chandni, you know how I once felt about you. I liked you even without knowing you. But things are different now and marriage is a different ballgame altogether. My parents were not expecting this proposal either. I will need some time to think it over.'

'Sure, Som,' replied Chandni. 'Take your time. But I don't want to lose a friend, whatever your decision may be. Can you promise me that?'

Som smiled. 'Yes, I promise,' he said.

IN DELHI, TANYA kept confined to her room. Who cared for the damned agency job? She was doing it just to be occupied and to get to be with Som every day. But after the revelation about Chandni, she could just not pretend to go on from one assignment to another. Bhaskaran had just sent her a message about the Bollywood night in Benares.

'Payal, tell Bhaskaran that I'm quitting. I don't like Delhi anymore and I'm going back to Pune,' Tanya was sobbing uncontrollably on the phone.

'What?' yelled Payal. 'What happened now? Has Som got married? How dare he do that!'

Payal called up Bhaskaran. 'Has Som accepted the marriage proposal?' she demanded.

Bhaskaran was eating a hot samosa. He almost burnt his tongue in trying to reply at once. Pausing a few seconds, he whispered into the phone. 'She is the most beautiful girl in town. But Som is not interested.'

Payal called back Tanya to give the good news. 'You'll be a perfect loser if you don't tell Som about your feelings now. By the time you gather courage, he'll be married and have a pot belly and four kids.'

Chastised in such a manner, Tanya felt even more enraged. Why did she have to be happy because Som had rejected the most beautiful girl on earth? Som had still not understood her love for him after all these months.

After a while, she calmed down.

'Mummy,' shouted Tanya. 'I have to go to Benares next week.'

In Kolkata, the suave Bhaskaran was regaling the Roy household with his tales from around the world. Even Chandni's teenage sister listened in rapt attention as Bhaskaran spoke about the adventurous Australia and romantic Paris.

That night, Som could not sleep from the stress of having to decide about Chandni.

'I'd better leave for Benares in a day or two. By the time my work there ends, I should be able to arrive at a decision,' he thought.

The next morning, Dr Vibhas Pandey called up. 'How are you, Som? Bhaskaran said you're travelling to Benares. There is this lodge I know at Gadaulia where you can stay for a few hundred rupees. The place is small but it's near the ghats. I can't ask Tanya to stay there but you will certainly enjoy the environs.'

'So kind of you, Sir,' Som said. He was happy that Tanya was coming.

He started to pack his bags.

'What's the matter now?' Ram Mukherjee asked. 'Where are you going?

'Baba, I have to go to Benares for a week or so. I will be back after that, in time for Durga Puja. Bhaskaran has promised that he won't disturb me then,' replied Som.

Savita was ecstatic that her son was going to a holy place. She duly instructed him to visit the ancient Shiva temple of Kashi Vishweshwar and give alms to beggars at the Dasaswamedh Ghat.

'May Lord Shiva relieve your mind of all worries and remove all obstacles from your path,' she blessed Som.

Four days passed.

Som had reached Benares by train and was comfortably ensconced in the lodge that Dr Pandey had recommended. He had liaised with a local event organiser and surveyed the spot for the show on the highway to Allahabad. All municipal and police clearances had been obtained and a tent was being erected. Tanya had checked in at a hotel in the city, and Payal was to join the next day with cine artists from Mumbai. Bhaskaran and Mr Aggarwal were due to come together from Kolkata.

Som was finishing his tea when Tanya called him. 'Where are you?' she asked.

Som felt good to hear Tanya's voice again. It was just a little more than a week since they had last spoken but it seemed like ages.

The two met outside the entrance to the Vishwanath Gali.

Tanya had wanted to offer prayers at the ancient Shiva shrine.

BACK IN THE Roy household, the air was rife with anticipation. 'Shona Ma,' Biswajeet called out to his daughter. Chandni knew that the moment of reckoning had arrived and she absolutely dreaded the outcome.

As Chandni sheepishly answered her father, he urged her to take a seat beside him.

The entire family had gathered in the living room. Garima and Basu were also present.

'So, what have you thought about your marriage?' Biswajeet asked.

'I will accept whatever you and ma decide,' Chandni replied, her head bent low.

'Are you sure, Chandni?' asked Biswajeet. 'We have already ruined your life once by making a wrong choice. Can you trust us?'

Chandni looked up. 'Why do you punish yourself? You have always wanted the best for me. It's just my bad fate that this happened.'

'Yes, and since then I have been fighting fate to rectify that mistake. I go from door to door and beg every son's father to accept our proposal. They think I am a mad man. But let it be so. I don't care. I will get you married and I will do it in style,' thundered Biswajeet Roy.

'Listen to me, you all. I have fixed Chandni's marriage. The groom and his parents have agreed on an auspicious date next month,' he continued.

Chandni covered her face with both hands and broke down. Everybody else in the room clapped roaringly.

Garima went over to Chandni and hugged her. Basu hugged Partho. Pinky jumped on her mother in joy.

Biswajeet added, 'The best part is that Chandni will live in the US and run her own dance academy there. The groom is a proud man. He has refused to accept anything for himself.'

Basu had tears in his eyes. 'I can't believe that Som had so much sense,' he said.

'Certainly not,' said Biswajeet. 'Som has no sense.'

IN BENARES, AFTER they had offered prayers at the Kashi Vishwanath temple, Tanya and Som walked towards the timeless Dasaswamedh

Ghat. The sight of the Ganges was simply mesmerising. Boats plied across her breadth, with pilgrims joining hands in reverence. At the numerous ghats lined on the bank, the priests and families had begun preparations for the evening *aarti*. Scores of little leafy lamps were afloat on the river.

'Tanya, why didn't you arrive earlier?' Som asked. 'We could have sat here all week like this.'

'It was my birthday yesterday. I couldn't have left mummy alone,' Tanya replied calmly.

Som was embarrassed. 'I am so sorry, Tanya. I completely forgot. I was actually so occupied in different …'

Tanya interrupted Som. 'Don't be sorry for anything. How is Chandni?' she changed the topic.

'She's fine,' he replied, still feeling ashamed.

They sat in silence for a few minutes, watching hundreds of people walk up and down the ghats. Some were getting a head massage done while others sat reciting *slokas*. Some were oiling their bodies while yet others were feeding the poor. It was like a fair of sorts.

'It's getting late. I have to take a rickshaw to town,' said Tanya as she got up suddenly.

Som could not say anything to stop her. She vanished beyond the stairs, into the darkness.

The phone rang. It was Basu.

'You loser,' screamed Basu. 'Your friend Bhaskaran is marrying the girl you once loved. He is selling the PR agency to some Saklani and moving to the US.'

Chapter 13

Confession

Som was shocked out of his wits.

It seemed that a heavy rock had fallen on his chest. His knees gave way and he slumped back on the stairs with a thud. It hurt.

The pain was not about losing Chandni. Som did not want to marry her. The pain was caused by the way Bhaskaran had toyed with him, his emotions and his career. Everything now stood destroyed.

The phone rang again.

It was now Payal's turn to lash out at Som. 'You idiot, it was you who invited Bhaskaran to Kolkata, right? You knew about our affair. If you didn't want to marry that bitch, why tempt your friend? I am not helping you now. You can forget about the event.' She was livid.

'I had no idea, Payal ....,' Som muttered. But she hung up.

Som threw his phone towards the river. It landed a hundred feet away and hit a monk walking up the stairs. The monk grabbed it quickly enough to not let it slip into the river.

Som stood up. What if the phone had hit the man hard?

He then somewhat recognised the face coming closer to him.

'You seem familiar,' said the monk, now just ten feet away from him.

'Yes. I think we met in a train over two years ago,' Som replied.

Swami Swarup Damodar Das blessed Som and signalled him to sit down. 'You seem healthier and wealthier now. So, why are you throwing things at others, my son?' the Swami asked.

Som was crestfallen. He poured out his heart to the wise monk, explaining how, in a single stroke, Bhaskaran had finished off the agency, the team and his career.

'Nothing is finished for those who follow the Lord. Think of the people who have stood steadfast by you. They are still there for you. And remember, success cannot be benchmarked. What matters is the happiness of the heart,' the swami advised.

The wise man then walked off.

The past fifteen months flashed in front of Som's eyes. He recalled how a despondent, fidgety Tanya had transformed into a confident, mature individual. How she had kept pace with him on long trips for press meets, ceremonies and functions. How she had always organised everything silently, even packing his stuff at times. And how she had never complained or despaired, even in the most trying of moments.

Som remembered how Tanya had tended to him when he had a high fever in Bangalore. She had refused to work, and had asked Payal to reschedule all media interviews for the client. But what did he do in Jaipur? He had carried on for the press meet with Chandni, leaving Tanya in the hotel room.

The events of his first day back in Kolkata came to his mind. Basu had ridiculed Som, saying that he perhaps needed a mad girl to get married. Som had argued, 'Yes, the girl has to be mad enough to follow me wherever I go, help me in whatever I do, and believe in whatever I live for. She should be able to board a train with me to nowhere and still be kicked about it!'

'Alright, Sir. You call me the day you find such a girl and I will pay for your marriage function. That's a deal,' Basu had promised.

Som got thinking. Of course, he knew one such mad girl. It was Tanya. Why did he not realise it earlier?

The next pillar of strength was Dr Vibhas Pandey. Som called him at once and related the whole incident.

'Don't worry, Somashish,' assured Dr Pandey. 'You fax me your resignation. I will accept it as the co-owner of the agency. That will absolve you of your duties, and Bhaskaran can handle the doomed event in Benares himself. You get Tanya out of there and reach Delhi immediately. Tell your local event manager that you've quit and they should collect their payments from Bhaskaran. I will tackle Saklani.'

Som understood. He typed a message to Bhaskaran: *I resign. Congratulations on the wedding. You could have told me yourself.*

There was no response from Bhaskaran.

Som packed his suitcase and went straight to the hotel where Tanya was put up. He enquired her room number at the reception, but was informed that she had already left for Delhi. So he wrote out a resignation letter and faxed it to Dr Pandey.

Som then called Tanya. 'Why did you just leave like that?' he asked.

'I can't play games like you and Bhaskaran,' she said. 'Moreover, I can't work with Ashish Saklani.'

Som proceeded to the railway station and took the next train to Delhi at four in the morning. On reaching there in the evening, he hired a cab to his Patparganj apartment, packed his belongings and drove out in his car.

Just after ITO, Som saw a black dog straying on the road. Driving at eighty kilometers an hour, he could not immediately apply the brakes. He honked loudly but it was too late by then. The car crashed against the dog and there was a loud noise. Som's head banged against the steering wheel.

In the next moment, everything became dark. Som felt a piercing pain run through his head, and he cried out instinctively. His body was shaken by the impact. He could not move for several seconds. As he struggled to regain senses and see beyond the darkness, he realised that he might have just escaped death. He looked at himself in the rear view mirror. A cut bled from the left side of his forehead. Som touched the spot and looked at his red fingers.

After a while, he got off to inspect the condition of the car and the dog. There was a small hole in the bumper of the size of the dog's tooth. But the dog had survived, miraculously. Soon, it got up and limped off into the by-lanes.

Som was still shaken. He sat down on a stone slab by the roadside.

THE DOORBELL RANG at eleven in the night. Tanya opened it. She was surprised to see Som. She had not expected him in the least.

Archie, Betty and Veronica had retired for the night with Mrs Sachdev. Jaggu started barking loudly upon seeing Som. The dog had never barked at him before. It seemed that it too was resentful at the misery caused to its mistress.

'What are you doing here?' she asked him sternly. 'It's quite late.'

Som had anticipated the cold reception.

'Can I have a glass of water, please?' he pleaded.

Pointing towards the fridge, she said, 'Please help yourself and kindly be gone now.'

Tanya walked off straight to her bedroom.

Som saw her disappear behind the curtains. There was a new awakening within him after the car crash. He was now acutely aware of how much he and Tanya meant to each other. Of how they had come inseparably close. And yet, he was such an idiot not to realise it all these months.

But it was not too late. He would not lose Tanya, not at any cost.

Som followed Tanya to her bedroom. He paced rapidly to come within reach and then grabbed her wrist. 'Please listen to me, Tanya. For God's sake!'

Tanya turned around in fury and planted a hard slap on Som's cheek.

The impact was such that it stunned Som for a moment.

Tanya was a burning cauldron. 'What do you think of yourself, Mr Somashish Mukherjee? You can play with me? Why did you think I was following you around the country for a year? Because Bhaskaran paid me lots of money? I was silly enough to indulge you but you are not an immature person. You knew that I liked you, and you both continued to use me and Payal. Please go back to your Chandni now. I am not her substitute,' she roared.

Som came closer and spoke slowly.

'I will now go from here, Tanya. But not without saying what I should have months ago.

'I have been such a dumb ass not to realise why you left your home, mother and everything else to just be with me wherever I went. You didn't need this job. But I needed you. I wouldn't have been successful without you. You cared for me just as a sweetheart would. And you loved me silently every moment on the way, neither expecting nor, indeed, getting any reward or retribution.

'I didn't realise I love you until today when I felt I'm going to lose you. When my car almost crashed today, I knew how close I was to death. It struck me that I might never meet you again. And my heart sank.

'Chandni and I were never lovers, not even friends. I liked her, and so did every other boy in college. It was a teenage crush that is so much a part of growing up. It had its own bitter ending but I don't feel for her what I feel for you. Which is why I didn't marry her. If there is anyone I love, it is you. There's nobody else in my life. I love you, Tanya,' declared Som. 'As for Bhaskaran, I have nothing to do with him anymore.'

'Get out of my house right now, you liar!' Tanya commanded. 'I know Bhaskaran has sent you here to placate me because you guys need me for the event.'

Som had nothing more to say. He had not expressed himself in so many words to anyone before. He turned back and slowly walked out of the house.

Tanya called up Payal. 'Som told me he loves me. And I slapped him.'

'Don't lose your man, Tanya,' Payal was relaxed. 'He's not like Bhaskaran. He's done nothing wrong. Dr Pandey told me everything. I romanced the wrong guy. It happens in life. I'll move on. There's this smart kid next door. He's really kind of sweet,' she said.

'You sound exactly like Bhaskaran,' Tanya was bewildered at Payal's sudden loss of anger.

She was now feeling really bad that she had hit Som for no reason.

In Kolkata, Som's parents were worried about his future. They were shocked by how Bhaskaran had won over Chandni's father but were glad to be rid of Biswajeet Roy. Chandni, on the other hand, was happy at the way things had turned out. She knew that Som's parents were not happy with her father and tensions were bound to hamper the marriage. On the other hand, Bhaskaran's parents apparently loved the idea of a daughter-in-law who knew bharat natyam.

'One thing I can't fathom,' Chandni told Bhaskaran, 'why is Som not taking my calls?'

'He is plain irresponsible,' Bhaskaran replied. 'He and his girlfriend, Tanya, ran back to Delhi because I am selling my stake in the agency. I had to cancel a Bollywood night in Benares because of their odd behaviour. It cost me seven lakh!'

Chandni smiled and said, 'I knew Tanya loved Som. But maybe Som himself did not know.'

'But Bhaskaran, Som is my friend. I will not get married unless he and Tanya attend the wedding. I don't care how you convince them,' she declared.

Biswajeet Roy agreed. 'Whatever my daughter says needs to be done.'

Bhaskaran was in a tight spot now.

KENNY AND APARNA were happy to hear from Som. 'Where the hell have you been, wretched soul?' Kenny chided.

Som could not hold back his tears. He went through the painful story once more.

'I have shifted out of Patparganj and the landlord can throw away Bhaskaran's belongings. I plan to sell my car in a day or two and then shift back home to Kolkata. I am done with Delhi,' he said.

'Just hold on a few days, Som,' requested Aparna. 'We are coming to Dwarka for Dussehra and we will do something for you. Don't say quits yet.'

It was half past eleven now and Som was sitting in his car outside Munirka.

Feeling hungry, he decided to venture into the dingy bylanes to search for grub. His feet took him towards the same house where he had spent the golden moments of his life with Kenny and Aparna. He looked up towards the terrace, where his room was.

'Aaj itne din baad tanne humari yaad aayi?' A harsh voice frightened Som.

Manju aunty stood behind him like a mountain. She must be returning from the buffalo shed, Som thought.

He was very happy to see her. He asked if he could spend two nights in the rooftop room. Aunty was more than accomodating and even brought him a few rotis and pickle to eat.

'After you left, I had put the room up on rent to a young married couple,' said Manju as Som gratefully gorged on the food.

She then went on to narrate the story of Leon and Bulbul.

Leon was a young lad from Manipur who had come to Delhi for his post-graduation. Bulbul was doing her BA from School of Correspondence Studies.

One day, they boarded the same bus from North Campus. The bus was overcrowded, leaning sharply towards the left. Near Kingsway Camp, the driver had to negotiate a sharp turn and the bus lost balance, toppling over. It was then that Leon had rescued an injured Bulbul and taken her to the nearby Government hospital.

The love story that began with blood ended with blood.

The couple dated each other and married against their parent's wishes. Bulbul's brothers soon found out their hide-out and forcibly took her home with them. Leon complained to the police but in vain. He was thrashed mercilessly, and a false kidnapping case was lodged against him. The constables called him 'chinky' and treated him like dung. Unable to bear the pain, Leon cut his wrists in jail and bled to death. Bulbul soon hanged herself.

Manju tried all that she could to bring the perpetrators to book. With the help of a local ACP, she got Bulbul's brothers arrested and the constables suspended. But it wasn't enough. Leon and Bulbul were not coming back.

'I did not put that room up on rent again. I just clean it every month,' she said, closing the door behind her.

The world was grappling with greater problems than mine, Som thought. Som felt sorry for the couple, and was now thankful to God for everything. He called Dr Pandey to tell him his whereabouts and then went to bed.

The room had a familiar musty smell. For a long time, Som could not sleep. He imagined he could hear human voices whispering in the dark. It seemed that the ghosts of Leon and Bulbul were running about in the terrace outside the room. As the hours passed by, a sweet voice sang in an unfamiliar language. But Som wasn't scared. He felt soothed and tranquil and passed into deep sleep.

The next day, he travelled all over Delhi to try and sell his car.

After hovering around second-hand car markets in central Delhi, he headed south. He almost struck a deal with a mechanic in Lajpat Nagar but then developed cold feet when he saw some goons entering the garage.

Fearing for his life, he turned the ignition and fled away.

After a day's futile search, Som returned tired and hungry to his Munirka shelter.

'Your friend has come to meet you. *Ib saadi kar le,*' Manju aunty winked.

Som found Dr Pandey and Tanya waiting in his rooftop refuge. 'You know, Tanya, this is the place from where Som started his struggle in Delhi,' Dr Pandey said.

After half an hour, the professor took leave. 'I'll see you tomorrow. I hope to have some good news by then,' he said.

Som looked at Tanya. 'Are you still angry with me?' he asked.

'Yes,' said Tanya. She walked up to him. 'Som, you will have to say sorry first.'

Som obeyed. 'I'm very sorry, Tanya,' he said.

Tanya was in tears. 'Then I'm sorry too. I slapped you and said so many things to you without thinking. There's nothing wrong with what you did. After all, I never told you about my feelings.'

Som looked at Tanya's puffy face. 'Don't be sorry for love,' he said. She was looking more chubby than usual. Her melancholic eyes seemed drunk from bouts of endless crying. If only the glasses would come off, he could have a closer look at them.

'What's that purple bruise on your forehead, Som?' asked Tanya. She came forward and examined the spot. 'You need some iodine,' she said.

'No, I just need you,' Som whispered.

In the moment that followed, Som drew Tanya by the waist and held her face close to his own. He removed her glasses to reveal the beautiful, expressive eyes. Her lips quivered as they looked into each others' eyes. Som softly kissed her forehead and then her eyebrows. Tanya shuddered instinctively and struggled, feebly, to break free.

But Som held her waist even more tightly, drawing her closer to him. She could not resist his warmth and desire. His touch was setting her on fire. She wanted him all over her being.

They embraced each other like two entwined creepers. He kissed her lips, slowly at first, and then with intense passion and longing. As their breaths merged, Tanya wished that Som would hold her thus till eternity. She would dissolve into him and find lasting peace and refuge in his golden heart, far from the pains of the world.

Som did not know what had seized him. He could not get to stop himself. His breathing was heavy, and he was going mad with pleasure. He loved the way Tanya smelled. It reminded him of fresh green apples. Her softness pressed against his manly frame, driving him crazy. He kissed her ears, slightly biting her earlobes. Tanya moaned. Som pushed her against the wall and then bent down to spray kisses on her cheeks, chin and neck. She flung her arms around his neck and played with his hair as his hands caressed her back and waist.

They were kissing deeply and for longer and longer.

Suddenly, Tanya noticed that the door was open. She pushed Som to the bed and ran to lock the door.

As she came back to Som, she switched off the lights.

Som took her in his lap. His fingers touched her bare belly, sending a chill up her body. She had undressed to the bare minimum, her gold bracelet and chain shimmering in the darkness. 'I love you, Som. Take me right now, right here. I can't wait for tomorrow to come. Please make me yours,' she said.

Suddenly, Som recalled the story of Swarna Prabha Yakshini that Vishambhar Narain Dutt had narrated on the tour to Rishikesh.

'You're a pucca chudail,' he said, smiling.

Tanya hit him on the nose. He caught her wrists and lay her down on the bed, showering her with kisses. He felt it his sacred duty to caress and kiss every inch of her body. He wanted to obliterate all distances between them. They had reached a point of no return.

And then, he remembered. 'I don't carry contraceptives,' he said. 'Neither do I,' said Tanya.

She laughed and threw her undergarments on the floor.

Chapter 14

Aftermath

Som woke up from the most satisfying sleep of his life. The events of the night were like a rapturous dream and he didn't want to emerge from the sea of bliss pervading his mind. Not yet.

But Tanya wasn't in bed. The door to the terrace was ajar and soft white light peered in through the edges.

Bleary-eyed, Som rolled over to the side where Tanya lay last night. The crumpled bedsheet was still warm from her touch, smelling of fresh green apples.

'I love you, Tanya,' Som whispered as his fingers caressed the sheet, hoping to find some remnant of her – a touch here, a breath there. But all he found was a small piece of yellowed newsprint.

He took a closer look. Tanya had scribbled something on it with a blunt pencil, maybe her eye liner.

'Luv U. Going to Payal's house. Ma thinks I'm there.'

Som smiled. He wondered what had got into him last night. Was it Leon's spirit that had possessed him and driven him out of his senses? He had never imagined sex before marriage. In fact, he wasn't prepared even for marriage until 2007 when he expected to be earning multiple times his current income.

But now he had no income, did he? He had just quit Bhaskaran's, or now Saklani's, PR agency, and was selling his car to move back to Kolkata! So where would his newfound love go from here? Did he make love to Tanya only to withdraw from her forever?

No, he had to think this out. Things had changed. Everything had changed.

Som's phone rang.

It was Payal.

'So, hero! How does it feel? Is Tanya hotter than me?' she teased him. Before he could reply, Tanya took the phone from Payal.

'Hi, sorry I had to leave. I had told Mummy that I'd spend the night at Payal's house,' she said shyly.

'Goodmorning,' said Som. He couldn't express what he felt. 'I am sorry I lost control ...' he began.

'Don't be sorry for anything, please.' Tanya stopped him midway through his regret speech. 'It was the most wonderful moment of my life,' she said.

'Som, I have already booked my ticket to Pune,' she continued. 'I have to fly out tomorrow. I'll be back only next month now. Can we meet at Vasant Kunj in the afternoon?'

Payal snatched the phone back. 'Call me when you miss her. I will remain in Delhi,' she burst out laughing.

'Are you always crazy, Payal?' Som freaked out.

Just as he had kept the phone down on the bed, Manju aunty flung the door open. Handing over a cup of tea to him, she said, '*Nigode, ib saadi kar le*. Unless you get married, I won't allow that girl to spend nights here. Marry her by law and you can stay here for free. Or I'll throw you out.'

'Yes, aunty,' said Som. 'But I need a job first.'

SOM AND TANYA met near the Vasant Kunj telephone exchange. It was Vijayadashami and the Durga puja festivities were coming to an end. In the nearby community hall, Bengali women were playfully smearing each other with vermillion, as if celebrating the divine feminity manisfest in each of them.

Tanya was mesmerised at the sight. 'Can I join them, Som?' she asked.

'No, you have to be married first to play with sindoor.'

But she did not pay heed. 'I'm already married and my God knows it,' she said, smiling, as she ran to join the crowd. The women were initially surprised to see a young lady, without any visible signs of matrimony, approach them. But one of them noticed a black-beaded chain on Tanya's neck. Thinking it to be a *mangalsutra*, she came forward and smilingly marked Tanya's forehead.

Amid the blowing of conchshells and beating of drums, Tanya was soon coloured in brilliant red. It was as if the Goddess had blessed her union with Som.

Meanwhile, Som stood pondering over the word 'married'. Was he really married now? And to a Punjabi girl?

He recalled how his mother had warned him of Punjabi girls before he left Kolkata almost three years ago. He realised that his family would not accept the 'marriage'. He was already doomed!

Many miles away at a five-star hotel, Ashish Saklani was engaged in an intense conversation with Dr Vibhas Pandey.

'Why don't you understand, Vibhas?' yelled Saklani. 'What will you achieve by stonewalling this deal? Bhaskaran has sold me his seventy per cent stake for seventy lakh. At that valuation, I will pay you thirty lakh for your thirty per cent holding. Take the money and join Adrenalin as an employee. I will make you the CEO,' he offered.

Dr Pandey was unmoved.

'Captain, I will not sell my stake and you will have to keep all the current employees if you want me to cooperate,' he asserted.

Saklani wasn't pleased. 'Look, I can think about keeping Som. Tanya has no place in my agency and so does Payal.'

'Then I'm afraid you will find a stumbling block in me,' Dr Pandey said in a grave voice.

Saklani was irritated.

'Look, Vibhas. There are ways in which I can wrest control and put you under curbs. But I don't understand how an academic like you repeatedly sacrifices his interests for a bunch of sissy clowns. Whatever do they mean to you?'

'My students and my colleagues have been my life, Ashish,' said Dr Pandey. 'And Tanya and Payal are like my daughters. But you won't understand. If you really did, you would not have sunk Thinking Caps in the first place.'

Saklani was outraged. 'Very well, professor,' he said. 'I then give you two choices. Sell me your shares by tomorrow and I'll sweeten the deal to thirty-five lakh. Or get ready to be physically evicted from the office. You can remain a shareholder but management control is with me. I will relieve you from your administrative position.'

Dr Pandey did not bat an eyelid and continued to glare at Saklani defiantly.

As he stood up to leave, Saklani had a last word of advice to offer. 'Don't oppose me in this small industry. Take my hand. You can't even imagine how big we can make it together.'

Dr Pandey replied, 'I have nothing personal against you, Ashish. But I have to take care of my kids.'

He sat back and watched Saklani hobble away to the hotel lobby. There was a deep desperation about the way Saklani wanted control of Testosterone. If he didn't want the talent pool, what else did he want? The client base was good and so was the turnover. One crore rupees was, in fact, a discounted price to pay for an agency that had so much goodwill as a niche events and projects player. But could his team service the clients as well as the cerebral and sincere trio of Som, Tanya and Payal?

And then, a sudden thought struck Dr Pandey. He immediately called Som.

'Som, you can return to your Patparganj home. Bhaskaran will send someone to collect his stuff. Also, be prepared to come to office tomorrow. I am selling my shares to Saklani and quitting. But he is recruiting you back,' Dr Pandey said.

'But Sir,' said Som. 'How will I survive there without you?'

'Don't worry. I need you to be there for some months until I figure out what Saklani is after. And you need the job.'

Som knew he needed a job if he were to stay in Delhi.

'What about Tanya and Payal? Tanya will not work for him anyways,' he expressed his concern.

'Don't worry. I will find some assignment to keep us busy until I figure out what to do next,' he assured.

Gathering his thoughts, Som resolved to make a fresh beginning with Saklani. Perhaps Ashish would not be harsh on him since he was the last person to quit Thinking Caps for Testosterone. Perhaps he would hit it off with Santosh Yadav once again. Whatever the circumstances, he would have to carry on regardless.

As Som packed his stuff into the car, firecrackers burst in the vicinity, heralding the victory of Lord Ram over Ravana – the triumph of good over evil.

IN KOLKATA, HIS mother arranged sweets on a plate as Rahul danced around like a demon, eager to devour the whole tray. Ram Mukherjee had a smile on his face after many days of stress over Som's uncertain future.

'This is the third running year that we didn't have Som with us for Durga Puja,' he remarked. 'Ask him to turn up for Kali Puja at least. He will get some holidays around Diwali, won't he?' he asked Savita.

'Yes, Som promised that he will speak to the new boss,' she said. 'And after the Chandni incident, I am not taking any chances. I have asked Chaitali to bring her daughter on Kali Puja so that Som can meet her. If all goes well, by God's grace, we will do an engagement ceremony.'

Ram was alarmed.

'You have chosen Som's bride even before he has met her? What if he doesn't like her?' he demanded.

'You don't have to worry about that,' replied Savita. 'Why won't Som like Tanusree? She cooks well, has done her BA in Bengali Literature, and sings excellent Rabindra Sangeet. And above all, Chaitali is my sister's best friend. They will always hold us in high esteem and not injure our pride like Biswajeet Roy.'

Rahul stopped dancing. He mocked his mother. 'You are marrying *dada* off to a chef and an item girl?'

'Stop talking about your sister-in-law like this. Take this plate and be gone, you little rascal,' ordered Savita.

Rahul descended on the sweets at once and began eating with both hands.

Ram and Savita laughed at him lovingly. Savita's eyes were joyous at the thought of her elder son's wedding. She could not wait to see Som and Tanusree together.

Back in Delhi, Som's maid servant, Reshma, was talking to an office peon outside the Patparganj apartment.

'Where is Bhaskaran, Sahib?' she demanded.

'He's sold the agency and gone forever,' Kalu replied. 'I have come to collect his belongings.'

'Why, what happened? He didn't like it?' she asked.

'Didn't like what?' Kalu was puzzled.

'No, I mean didn't he like Delhi?' clarified Reshma. 'He is a Madrasi, isn't he?'

'Yes, he was from Chennai but had been living in Delhi since a long time,' said Kalu. 'He found a beautiful Bengali girl to marry.'

Reshma swallowed.

'Is she very beautiful? More beautiful than me?'

Kalu was surprised at her question. The frown on his forehead slowly gave way to a glad stretch. 'You are a firecracker. How can anyone be better than you?'

AT THE MORNING briefing the next day, Ashish Saklani occupied Dr Vibhas Pandey's seat.

Old faces, Santosh Yadav and Prem Rawat, sat by his side. Ejaz Ahmed and Raghu Pillai sat in a corner. There were two unknown people – both girls.

Saklani addressed Som directly.

'We have come a full circle, Som. When I hired you and Bhaskaran almost one-and-a-half years ago, little did I realise what damage that baboon could do to my agency. But I had faith in you. You could have alerted me in time. But you played ball with them. What did you think you would achieve? It is not easy to defeat me. What are you guys? Mere babes. You think you have become a top-notch PR professional by pulling off a few events? The clients you have today do not trust you enough to pay retainer fees. A Mittal or a Thapar would not even talk to you if you meet them. Isn't it, Santosh?'

Santosh smirked. Prem stared at Som like a hungry hyena. Contempt was writ large on Raghu's face.

Saklani wasn't done yet.

'Som, the reason I agreed to keep you after the professor pleaded with me is that we need to understand where the projects are and what false commitments that slimeball friend of yours has made. You will report to Ejaz and sort out the projects in a month. After that, we will see what to do with you,' he said.

It was the most humiliating moment of Som's life. He prayed for instant death.

Not even in his wildest dreams had he imagined that Saklani would treat him thus. All this had happened thanks to Bhaskaran. The scumbag had always been queer and wily, but the way he grabbed Chandni's wealth and sold out to Saklani was pathetic. It was a stab in the back. A shameful deceit!

Som lowered his head in indignation as everyone stood to leave the room. Ejaz patted on his shoulder and said, 'Let's sit in fifteen minutes. I have a call.'

Som diạlled Bhaskaran's number in anger. There was no response.

He tried many times but nobody picked up. Exasperated, he finally gave up.

In the ensuing silence, he could hear Santosh talk loudly on phone to someone in the next room.

'We have made all preparations. Ejaz will ensure that the existing clients stay back for some time until we move to the next phase. We need to focus on the work in the four states now. We need some visible action.'

Can't take the humiliation. I am quitting – Som sent an anguished SMS to Dr Pandey.

The reply was instantaneous: *For the sake of us all, please hang in there. We must know what Saklani is upto. My shares are still with me.*

Chapter 15

Two Generals

Tanya's mother stood surveying the garden outside her apartment.

It would soon be the onset of winter and the right time to plant some tulips and chrysanthemums, she thought. The green patch had been carefully nurtured by Bahadur under her watchful eye. It had taken over two months to gradually clear the concrete debris left by the municipality, and enrich the soil by mixing cowdung and manure in the right proportion.

Mrs Sachdev was pleased with herself and made up her mind to pick some seeds from the Aurobindo Ashram. As she turned to go back into the house, her eyes fell on a row of marigolds towards the outer side of the lawns. A few plants had drooped down to the earth, broken at their stems by the impact of something heavy. The leaves were pressed into the ground as if a tyre had run over them.

'Bahadur', she cried out. At once, the puny gardener-by-morning and driver-by-day emerged from the garage.

'Who has killed my plants there?' the lady of the house demanded.

Scratching his head a couple of times and looking fearfully at the scene of murder, Bahadur struggled for the right words.

'*Tod diya,* Memshaab', he mumbled.

Mrs Sachdev lost it. 'I know they are crushed, idiot! But who did this?'

Bahadur trembled at the thunderous outburst. He looked nervously to his right and his left and then to the sky. 'Yes, THEY did this', he revealed finally.

'Are you now drinking in the day also?' Mrs Sachdev was now yelling. 'I had told Colonel Sachdev not to spoil you with the canteen rum. And see, what has happened now.'

Bahadur gulped. 'Not a drop, Memshaab, I swear. Those Bengalis did it.' He pointed to the third-floor apartment of the opposite building.

'The Babu parks his car by our garden at night and leaves early every morning.' Bahadur concluded.

Mrs Sachdev put her hands on her waist and stared above angrily.

THE SKY WAS an azure blue. Lake Geneva was bustling with activity. Couples strolled along the walkways lined with trees, children on roller skates meandered through the crowd, and countless boats swarmed the lakeshore.

Ashish Saklani and Santosh Yadav sat at a bus stop at Rue de Mont Blanc, licking ice cream. It was very cold, indeed, but that did not deter them from enjoying a choco slush bonanza.

With his eyes half-closed, Saklani spoke slowly. 'You know, Santosh, this deal is bigger to me than my life. And you should treat it in the same manner. Even one small mistake will cost us dearly. I cannot afford failure. Not at the cost of the seventy-odd lakh that I paid to that maverick Bhaskaran.'

'Don't worry, captain,' assured Santosh. 'Why should we fail? After we acquired Testosterone, there is no other PR agency that can match us in terms of this kind of project execution across India,' he said.

'You don't get the point, Santosh,' said Saklani.

'Geoffrey Hampstead is the COO of America's largest public affairs firm. He will not be so casual when it comes to buying an Indian agency. He'll be more worried about not sinking his reputation than about the ten million dollar project. If Geoffrey gets an impression that Dr Pandey is not with us or our clients are unhappy, he will not buy me,' he explained.

Nibbling off the remains of the ice cream cone, Saklani continued, 'And we have Andreas Schneider from the Baumann Foundation who will ensure that every dollar of their grant is spent wisely.'

Wiping his mouth off, Saklani summarised, 'Even a million dollars is big money for us.'

Rising from the bench, he remarked as an afterthought, 'Call Ejaz and tell him to let Som go on a short vacation. Let that boy be happy and not suspicious of our plans.' Santosh nodded in obedience.

A few minutes later, the two boarded a tram to the United Nations headquarters.

At the appointed time, they found Geoffrey and Andreas, emerging from inside the black iron gates. The flags of different countries fluttered behind them in the chilly wind.

Santosh felt both nervous and excited. The presentation that he was to make to the EPP public affairs team and to Baumann Foundation was like a do-or-die battle.

He had to convince them that Adrenalin-Testosterone had the necessary scale and skill to mobilise public opinion and action to prevent malnutrition deaths in the poorest districts of India.

Santosh was confident about the two-year campaign plan that he had devised, but was not so about Testosterone's previous social advocacy projects. Som had, of course, given him a detailed brief on a number of such projects executed in partnership with small-time agencies, but it was not the same as doing it personally.

WITH ONLY A few days to go for Diwali, Som was happy that he would finally spend Kali Puja at his home – after three long years.

He wished that Bhaskaran and Chandni were already married and out of the city. He would not like to bump into them. Certainly not after how Bhaskaran ruined his career and left him at Saklani's mercy.

It had been a painful week at the new, consolidated agency with everyone except Ejaz behaving rudely with him.

It was also Ejaz who got the leave sanctioned.

As Som packed his bag to leave for the day, Prem Rawat gave him a menacing look.

Som felt like going across and grabbing Rawat by the scruff of his neck and asking him, 'What the shit on earth have you done to stare at me like that? Do you even know how to write a press release?'

And then, Som's phone rang. 'How's my Somu doing?' Tanya whispered at the other end. Som liked the way she said 'my' but hated the endearment 'Somu'.

'Listen, Somu sounds like that second-grader who did potty in his pants. Please call me something else,' he pleaded.

'Okay, I'll call you Somji,' Tanya giggled.

'It sounds Gujarati but it's better,' Som acquised.

'So, what's up, Somji?'

'Going back to Kolkata tomorrow. Will be there until a few days after Diwali. Ejaz got the leave sanctioned this morning.'

Tanya became silent for a while. For some unknown reason, Kolkata sounded an alert in her mind. She then said, 'I don't like Pune anymore. My maternal uncle is in Mumbai for an assignment. Aunty and I get bored all day. I want to come to Kolkata, I want to be with you. I miss you sooooo much!'

'I miss you too, Tanu,' said Som. 'Life hasn't been the same without you. Not after that night.'

'Shut up, don't embarrass me,' she said.

'I've told aunty everything. She's promised to help me but was worried that Bengali mothers-in-law and Punjabi *bahus* don't get along too well,' she added.

Som suddenly became serious. He had not yet thought about how he would break the news to his parents. It was an impending catastrophe, he knew.

There was gloom and despair at the Roy household.

Biswajeet Roy was crestfallen. His son, Partho, was pacing up and down the living room, arguing with his mother.

'I told Baba several times that we need at least one crore worth insurance. Look where we are now. The entire supermarket is gutted in fire and we are covered only for fifty lakh. Forget rebuilding the place, how will we buy Chandni anything in America now?'

On the terrace, Chandni and Bhaskaran sat motionless.

Tears flowed down Chandni's cheeks, wetting her saree.

'I don't understand how this happened,' Bhaskaran was bewildered. 'Two days to our engagement and somebody sets fire to your father's supermarket! And you had an apology of an insurance!'

'I understand that this may be the end of the American dream for you. I know it meant a lot to you,' Chandni said wryly.

With a straight face and looking into Bhaskaran's eyes, she continued, 'If you can betray a friend like Som for this dream, you can very well leave me, Mr CEO. I release you from this bondage. Please go back to Delhi.'

WHILE IT WAS doomsday for Bhaskaran in Kolkata, Saklani and Santosh Yadav were readying themselves for a long presentation to the EPP-Baumann Foundation team at the historic Bristol Hotel in Geneva.

They did not have an adaptor for their laptop and were worried they would run out of charge in an hour.

Just then, Saklani got a message on his cellphone.

'Santosh!' exclaimed Saklani. 'We have good news. Dr Pandey is selling his stake to me for thirty-five lakh. It can't go wrong from here on. It just can't!'

Santosh hugged Saklani in delight. 'Congratulations, general!'

Far away from the jubiliation, thousands of miles away at the Delhi airport, a voice called out at Terminal 1A.

'Somashish, wait for me!'

Som stopped dead in his tracks and looked behind. It was Dr Pandey running in past the entry gate. He was dragging a very large suitcase.

Som wondered what on earth was going on. He walked several paces to meet the professor midway in the hall.

'What's up, Sir?' Som was worried.

Dr Pandey was out of breath. He smiled and winked and put a hand on Som's shoulder.

'I'm coming with you to Kolkata. Raja Ghoshal, our local partner there, called me this morning. Saklani is upto something very big. He offered to pay Raja thirty lakh for six month's work,' said Dr Pandey.

Som was out of his wits. 'Why would they send me on vacation and plan a project in my home town?' he wondered aloud.

The professor removed his spectacles and grimaced. Narrowing his eyes, he asked bluntly, 'Do you trust me, Som? Will you do as I tell you?'

'Yes, general. Unto death,' Som promised, smiling.

'No Som, you have to be the general. You have to take back what is yours,' said Dr Pandey.

Chapter 16

War

Mrs Sachdev was furious.

'*Main keya*, look at the audacity of these people. First they drive their car over my plants and then come to my house telling me that I'm a land grabber!' she told Tanya on the phone.

'Chill, Mummy. Why are you so worked up over a few plants?' Tanya tried to cool her down.

'No, no beta. I'm going to take this very seriously,' Mrs Sachdev resolved.

'I will tell Pathak to throw these people out of the colony. You don't know what they said to me. They said Punjabis think paneer is a vegetable! When I told them that I will approach the RWA President, Banerjee said I should not show a Bengali the road to the High Court!'

Tanya guffawed but quickly recovered herself. She knew that her mother suffered from high blood pressure and any kind of stress was not good for her.

'Relax, Ma. I will speak to Pathak uncle. And you tell Bahadur to gather some thorny bushes to hedge the garden.'

'Whatever. I'm now so disgusted that I wonder if all Bengalis are crazy. Are Som's parents also like that?'

Tanya was taken aback for a moment. She had no answer. But she had to get one soon.

SAVITA MUKHERJEE WAS happy to see Som again after the past month's tumultous events. Her son had first lost a prospective bride and then his job. She now felt more responsible for ensuring that, at least, his personal life was on track.

Som had persuaded Dr Vibhas Pandey to stay with him, at the Mukherjee residence in Behala. And although Ram Mukherjee was, at first, wary of the new guest, he was soon relieved to know that the professor wasn't another groom-chaser like Biswajeet Roy.

In the evening, by the pond, Ram addressed Dr Pandey. 'I guess life is far more complicated today than it was in our times. Look at Somashish and the way he moves around the country doing something that my ancestors would not even understand,' he said.

Dr Pandey smiled.

Ram continued. 'People like me have been left behind with the times. I grew up in this dilapidated house, went to the only college in this part of the city, and then married the girl my father chose for me. For thirty years, I worked in the same company. I now look at you and these young boys who are beyond the limits of time and space and I feel completely left behind!'

'You are not, Mr Mukherjee,' assured Dr Pandey.

Gesturing towards the wild ducks padding in the pond, he said, 'I too grew up with ducks and buffaloes in my village outside Patna. The most enduring memory of my childhood was my mother standing in knee-deep water, praying to the Sun God with her eyes closed. The peace and joy that I felt to see her face gives me the confidence and strength to take on the vagaries of life even to this day.'

He continued, 'It is true that science and technology have bridged people and distances, though sometimes even to devastating effect. Social norms, cultures and beliefs are under constant pressure in this cacophony of unfamiliar voices. But that doesn't make old people obsolete. It allows us a chance to evaluate contrarian views for their inherent worth and imbibe the changes that are good for future generations.'

The conversation went on beyond dusk.

Meanwhile, Som was collecing more information from Raja Ghoshal.

It turned out that Saklani had personally called Raja from an international number to inform about Testosterone's takeover and offered him a monthly fee of five lakh rupees for some philanthropic work in the state's East Midnapore district.

Raja was at first aghast at the offer, but later thought that he should check with Dr Pandey if the project needed him to devote an extensive amount of time outside Kolkata.

Som dialled all his contacts in Orissa, Punjab, UP, Bihar, Maharashtra and South India. It seemed that at least three more calls had been made to their local PR partners in Maharashtra, Orissa and Tamil Nadu. In all cases, either Saklani or Santosh Yadav had made the calls, offering an extendable six-month exclusive contract for twenty-five to thirty lakh.

At the dinner table, Som briefed Dr Pandey about his findings. While the professor and his disciple talked, Ram looked at his son with newfound admiration. Though much of the conversation did not make sense to him, he was willing to help in whatever way he could.

'It is now abundantly clear why Saklani bought Testosterone. The venture capitalist that he essentially is, he has found an international organisation that is funding a mass-scale project in rural India and needs a good PR agency as a conduit. Adrenalin would have never got the contract had Testoterone not been sold. Between Som, Payal, Tanya and our local city contacts, we had the richest project experience among all agencies in India. And Saklani knew that, which is why he bought us. Only if Bhaskaran had not sold us!' Dr Pandey lamented.

'He's now repenting for whatever he did,' boomed a loud voice.

It was Basu in his inimitable style, arriving unannounced, walking through the front door that was always open until late night.

Basu regaled them with the somewhat tragic tale of Bhaskaran's shattered American dream.

'So, what happens to Chandni? I'm sure Bhaskaran will not marry her now,' Som was concerned.

'You'll be surprised to know, Som,' said Basu, 'that this may be a case of true love after all. Bhaskaran is so smitten by Chandni that he's not leaving her. But he's already paid forty lakh to his parents as loan repayment and is left with thirty lakh and no job,' Basu chuckled.

'In fact, it is Biswajeet Roy who regrets that he doesn't have a super-rich NRI groom for his daughter who could have bailed them out,' he said.

Ram was visibly upset. 'Why would anyone play with his daughter's life like this, I don't understand. That man was earlier ready to marry her off to any available boy and now she becomes his insurance?'

Dr Pandey grimaced.

'I will talk to Bhaskaran. Can he meet us here?' Som asked.

'I would think so,' Basu replied.

'Good,' said Dr Pandey. 'Som, can you call Tanya and ask her if she can fly down here? I will speak to Payal. If all goes well, I will get thirty-five lakh in my account from the stake sale to Saklani. If we get some more money, we can turn around our fortunes,' he added.

'I have five lakh from the cheques Som sent me over the two years and some personal savings. Please use it,' said Ram, touching Dr Pandey's hand.

'I have a cash surplus. I can loan out ten lakh for three-four months if you want,' proposed Basu.

Dr Pandey was elated.

BHASKARAN WAS HOLDING Chandni's hands and standing very close to her. 'Please try to understand me, honey. I did what I did because I wanted a future with you, far away from this land. Your father had dreamt of an American dance school for you and I was merely facilitating it by wrapping up my business here,' he said.

Chandni pushed him away.

'I don't know what to do now with you and my father. He called up Ashok Kumar's relatives today in the hope that the guy is still unmarried. It's disgusting!' Chandni cried out.

'Then forget him. Take my hand and come with me to Delhi. Something will work out, I'm sure. I'll beg Saklani to employ me in my own agency,' urged Bhaskaran.

Chandni was unmoved.

'I'd rather have you call Som and apologise to him than fall at Saklani's feet,' she said.

Bhaskaran was stunned but said, 'If that will make you marry me, I will do it.'

Chandni wiped her tears and looked at Bhaskaran threateningly.

'I don't know why I fell in love with a rascal like you. And to think that the entire college wanted to marry me!'

Bhaskaran laughed and drew her close. They locked lips.

Chandni did not know what drew her so passionately close to this man. It was a fatal attraction to something in Bhaskaran that was impervious, unpredictable, even dangerous. All these years of mental conditioning and subjugation to conventions and traditions could not prevent Chandni from falling deeper and deeper in love with this dark, intense man.

'Let me go home now,' Chandni pushed back her lover.

IN BEHALA, SOM was issuing instructions to his army before he slept.

'Listen carefully, Raja. You will bargain with Saklani and agree to a price of seven lakh a month. Ask him on whose name the contract will be signed and report back to me,' he ordered.

Dr Pandey turned to Som and said, 'After Payal and Tanya check in at the hotel tomorrow, tell them to call all the existing clients and mention that the entire Testosterone team has reorganised under a new name and we will inform them formally by fax.'

Som smiled nervously. He was happy that he would meet Tanya but was apprehensive that his parents might not be so to see her.

Chapter 17

Secret in a Saree

It was Diwali, or Kali Puja as it is observed in Kolkata. Tanya looked at the chaotic traffic outside from her taxi window. A battle was raging between two rickety buses to outspeed each other. Scores of cycles dodged around like players in a football field, miraculously avoiding collisions. The road from the airport to the city looked like it led into the interiors of some backward district.

'Which century is this? What place is this?' Payal asked Tanya in a mock shock.

But Tanya was not bothered. She had banished from her mind all the scepticism about Bengalis and Kolkata, and even her mother's quarrel with the Banerjees could not come in the way of her willingness to embrace everything related to Som.

And then, the landscape changed suddenly. Broad roads with signages and flyovers came into view. Policemen in spotless white clothes stood on guard at traffic intersections. And some modern, concrete and glass buildings dotted the horizon.

While Tanya looked on with the wondrous amazement of a newly wed who is sent to her new home, Payal sprayed on a perfume to repel the stench of tobacco pervading the taxi.

'Are you carrying a saree in your luggage by any chance?' Tanya asked Payal. Payal's eyes almost popped out of sockets.

'Don't tell me you want to gyrate like a heroine before Som's parents.' Payal sounded scandalised.

'Don't be nasty,' Tanya protested. 'I'm just trying to avoid wearing jeans when I meet them for the first time. I hadn't taken even a salwaar kameez to Pune. How would I have expected to be in Kolkata of all places suddenly?'

Payal's lips curled up in a naughty smile. 'I do have a saree. But the blouse may be too small for you now,' she said.

Tanya hit Payal hard with her leather bag.

IN BEHALA, SAVITA was chopping brinjals in the kitchen when a maid servant came running in with a message.

'Didi, Chaitali madam said that Tanusree will come in the evening with a friend,' she announced.

Savita was happy. She had planned an innocuous meeting between Som and Tanusree to see if they liked each other.

She folded her palms together and whispered a little prayer to Goddess Kali, urging her to bless Som's marriage.

Meanwhile, Som's bedroom now resembled a war room with Ram, Som, Dr Pandey, Basu and Bhaskaran all huddled together, skimming through dozens of documents typed on stamp paper.

Endless cups of tea lay on the floor under the bed.

'What is to be done now, general?' Dr Pandey asked Som.

'You tell us, Sir,' Som submitted.

The professor looked unusually tired from the hard work of the past twenty-four hours. But he managed a smile.

'Gentlemen,' he said. 'Everything is going as per our plan. Payal and Tanya are calling up our clients, greeting them on Diwali and telling them that we are a new company now.'

'Once all of us sign these agreements, we will become directors of this new agency called "One Up Masters", operating out of Raja's Kolkata office. As the biggest shareholder, I will be the MD and nominate Som as the CEO. Any objections, Bhaskaran?' Dr Pandey looked at him.

Bhaskaran shook his head, 'How can I object, Sir? Thanks to you, I still have half-a-chance to redeem myself.'

Basu smirked. Som was quiet but somehow believed Bhaskaran. 'The guy really loves Chandni,' he thought. 'I've never seen him so attentive and serious.'

'OK then,' said Dr Pandey. 'By evening, this letter will be faxed to all the clients. Som, can you read aloud what you have written, please?'

Som took the sheet of paper and read it aloud:

'Dear Mr XYZ,

At the very outset, please accept our warmest wishes on the festive occasion of Deepawali.

We take this opportunity to thank you for your kind patronage and support extended to us over the past fifteen months. It has been an exhilarating journey for us as we crossed many milestones together.

We have always been your biggest brand ambassadors, treating your business as our very own.

As we turn a new leaf today, we wish to inform you that the entire Testosterone team, as you knew us, has quit the company and formed a new PR agency called One Up Masters.
This dramatic, unprecedented action was necessitated by the takeover of Testosterone's assets by a rival company, Adrenalin, whose owner did not subscribe to the customer and employee-oriented policies of the previous management.

Therefore, in the best interests of our people and clients, we decided to break away and start afresh. We look to serving you with a renewed vigour and commitment, and an even bigger network of exclusive resources spread across different states.
We hope that you would reexamine your contract with Testosterone in the context of changed circumstances and appoint One Up Masters as your PR advisors.

While you are the true master of your decision, let us assure you that we will exceed your expectations when we work with you again.

Always at your service,

Yours sincerely,

Somashish Mukherjee
CEO'

'Bhaskaran, you will start faxing these letters at seven p.m.,' said Dr Pandey. 'Som, you will email your resignation letter to Saklani around the same time.'

'And now, Raja, please tell others what Santosh Yadav told you this morning,' he urged.

Raja Ghoshal coughed a few times before narrating the telephone conversation.

'Santosh said he was in Switzerland for a business meeting and Saklani is fine with an exclusive retainer fee of seven lakh per month. The contract, he said, should be with EPP Public Affairs India Pvt Ltd based in Delhi. And then he mentioned something about out-of-pocket expenses billed separately to some Boatman Foundation. That's all.'

Dr Pandey interjected. 'So, it is clear that the EPP Group is buying the agency from Saklani. And this philanthropy project is funded by this Swiss Foundation,' he said. 'I reckon that it is the Baumann Foundation and not Boatman Foundation. Mr Volker Baumann was a Swiss explorer and absolutely in love with India and its people,' he informed.

'How do we prevent EPP and the Swiss from trusting Saklani? Forget what happens to us, but the money meant for poor tribals will be siphoned off to that man's account!' complained Ram Mukherjee.

'No, uncle. Saklani is just the operative here. I have a feeling that a criminal is funding Saklani,' said Bhaskaran.

'Why didn't you tell us before?' Som shouted.

'I wasn't sure,' explained Bhaskaran. 'The seventy lakh cash that I received from Saklani was delivered by a man from Rishikesh. He seemed familiar but I didn't bother then. It just occurred to me that I had seen this fellow in the K Corp office in Delhi. He was Kathuria's peon. The same Kathuria who was jailed for a year for financial fraud.'

'Oh yes, the man is now out and wants to regain all that he had lost,' exclaimed Som. 'And he found a willing partner in Saklani who was devastated after we quit Thinking Caps.'

'We will not allow this deal to go through,' asserted Dr Pandey.

Som had an idea. 'Sir, please help me draft a letter to the COO of EPP Group. The only way we can get his attention is by claiming to be THE best projects PR agency in India, and proposing an alliance. As he must be getting offers for buying Indian agencies all the time, we will do something extraordinary!'

'Like what?' asked Dr Pandey.

Som had a twinkle in his eyes. 'We will propose to buy one per cent stake in HIS company and share half of the profits from all business referred by him. The offer will be impossible to resist. Instead of having to buy something, he will gain money and find resources to execute the project in India.'

'Bravo Som, bravo!' clapped Basu.

'Thank you. But do you know someone in Rishikesh who can give us a report on where Kathuria is and what exactly he is doing?' asked Som.

'Sure Sir, why not?' beamed Basu.

The group was jubiliant and everybody except Dr Pandey stood up.

'What happened, Dr Pandey?' Ram asked.

'There is one last but most important task,' Dr Pandey said. 'Our corpus, including Raja's five lakh, is eighty-five lakh. If we get three more parties contributing five lakh each, we can get to one crore. That is the money required to buy one per cent stake in EPP. They must be worth at least twenty million dollars.'

'Yes, I wasn't too sure about the valuation after currency exchange calculation,' realised Som.

'I have an idea,' said Raja. 'I will speak to our partners in Orissa, Maharashtra and Tamil Nadu. If they come on board, it will also ensure that Saklani cannot implement the project.'

'Why would they agree?' asked Basu.

'Because as a partner they will gain more than just retainer fees for six months,' Som replied.

It was eight in the evening, and Dr Pandey's team had completed all the tasks and gathered at the local Kali temple near Som's house for puja.

While Som was worried that Tanya and Payal had not yet reached, Savita stood at the altar with flowers in her hand, wondering where Tanusree had disappeared.

The temple priest was offering prayers, reciting potent mantras from *Sri Sri Chandi*, an ancient compilation of Sanskrit texts dedicated to the divine mother.

Just then, someone touched Savita's feet. 'No, no, not in front of ma,' Savita reacted instinctively.

'This is Chandni, aunty,' said Bhaskaran. 'Please bless us.' Savita pulled up the girl by her shoulders to reveal a beautiful moon-like face.

'May God bless you. You look so good together,' Savita said.

The three of them stood together, waiting to offer flowers to the deity.

Som crept up on Savita's left, too hurried to notice Chandni.

'Ma, there is somebody here to see you. Meet Tanu,' Som whispered into his mother's ears.

At once, Savita's face lit up. She smiled at Som and turned around to look at the tall, fair girl in a Mysore silk saree.

Tanya looked transformed. With kohl-lined eyes and a bindi on her forehead, she looked like a Goddess. Behind her stood Payal, also in a saree.

Savita hadn't seen Tanusree since the latter was eight years old. Assuming that Tanu meant Tanusree, she drew Tanya to her bosom.

Tanya's eyes welled up. So did Som's.

The priest urged the devotees to chant after him.

Om Jayanti Mangala Kali, Bhadra Kali Kapalini.

Chapter 18

Key Message

It wasn't before the proceedings ended that the dimunitive maid servant appeared before a surprised Savita. 'Chaitali di says that Tanusree is unwell. She has called you to their house tomorrow,' reported the maid.

Savita stood in utter disbelief. If Tanusree was unwell then who was this girl whom Som had introduced as Tanu?'

A few yards away, Dr Pandey was busy introducing Payal and Tanya to Ram, Raja and Basu. Savita was perplexed and confused but decided to move away quietly. Meanwhile, alerted by Payal's presence, Bhaskaran was trying to whisk Chandni off.

'I am not going anywhere,' protested Chandni. 'Look at this message from Baba: *Good news, Ashok Kumar is now divorced from the Brazalian.* This is really disgusting. I'm not going back to that house again.'

Bhaskaran pulled Chandni to a corner and called out for Som.

'What's the matter?' asked Som. He was too preoccupied in witnessing how his father interacted with Tanya.

'Listen Som, we have a problem here. I need to marry Chandni. Right now,' said Bhaskaran, with a straight face.

'Are you nuts or what?' Som was stupefied.

Basu overheard the conversation.

'Listen, come home with me, both of you,' he said to Bhaskaran. 'Garima will call Chandni's home to inform.'

While the others were in conversation, the three of them walked away into the night.

THE NEXT MORNING, Som awoke quite late.

Dr Pandey was gone, having shifted to a guest house near Raja Ghoshal's office – the new headquarters of One Up Masters.

Tanya and Payal had left late last night and Som had requested Raja to escort them back to their hotel.

And Bhaskaran and Chandni had followed Basu to his house.

All was quiet now.

Som lay reflecting on the past few days. He prayed that their gamble paid off and that he had a job and career again.

It was in this very room that he once had resolved to benchmark himself against the best and earn thirty lakh rupees by 2007. While he was not even halfway there, he did have a girlfriend now and marriage, whenever it came, was sure to be a long-drawn complicated affair.

A rustle in the room broke his chain of thoughts. It was his mother, freshly bathed and dressed, holding in her hand a plate of offerings from her morning worship.

'Som, tell me the truth and nothing but the absolute truth,' she said, without wasting any time. 'What is your relationship with the girl you called Tanu?'

AT THE HOTEL in Shakerpeare Sarani, Tanya was shedding large tears. 'What the hell has happened to you,' a red-eyed Payal demanded.

Tanya did not answer. She dug her face deep into her knees and shook her head. 'I can't tell Som.'

Payal didn't have the patience to endure all the sobbing and drama. 'Did Som's mother say something nasty to you? Shall I speak to Som?' she asked firmly.

'No, please don't,' reacted Tanya.

'Aunty is very loving. But what do I do about this now?' she said, picking up a little piece of plastic.

'What the hell! Don't tell me you're pregnant!'

IN GENEVA, SAKLANI and Santosh were enjoying dinner. The lavish spread included roasted duck with boiled veggies, and an assortment of breads and wines.

'Santosh, well done, my boy. I am proud of you. Take some days off once we reach India tomorrow,' said Saklani. 'You need to recharge your batteries. The work begins in two weeks.'

Just then, Geoffrey Hampstead walked in with Andreas Schneider. They came straight towards the table where Saklani and Santosh sat.

'May we join you, gentlemen?' asked Geoffrey, in a tone that sounded more of an instruction than a request.

Santosh quickly rearranged the chairs. 'Certainly, Sir,' he said.

Geoffrey had a deep frown on his forehead. Andreas wore the same deadpan look, betraying no emotion.

'You see, I thought that I had reached a conclusion about buying your agency and letting you handle Baumann's project, but that's not the case anymore. I'm sorry to disappoint you but there are several facts which have come to light today that disqualify you from the process,' said Geoffrey.

Saklani put the fork down on his plate.

'For one, you are not the top projects PR agency in India, although you have bought the physical assets of your top rival. You have retained neither the talent nor the clients of that agency called Testosterone. Even the local resources in our target states are not with you.

'Secondly, you have funded your acquisition through the tainted money of a fraudster who lives in a Himalayan ashram and who, allegedly, runs an escort service for politicians and bigwigs,' admonished Geoffrey.

'This is utter nonsense. What proof do you have of the insinuations you make?' roared Saklani.

Andreas finally opened his mouth. 'Easy, boy. We got a letter from Mr Somashish Mukherjee and testaments by Dr Vibhas Pandey and Mr Bhaskaran. The Swiss police have also checked your antecedents. You made the last call to Rishikesh only yesterday.'

'Be relieved that you are going scot-free after attempting to mislead us about your credentials and capabilities. Be thankful to Swiss hospitality,' concluded Andreas.

HOURS BEFORE THE bomb dropped on Saklani, there was a fair-like festivity at Kalighat in Kolkata. The temple bells rang out every now and then. A sea of people thronged the premises to partake in the divine offerings of the previous night.

Two couples were conspicuosly dressed in traditional Bengali garments. Basu and Garima had commissioned a priest to perform the marriage of Bhaskaran with Chandni and of Som with Tanya. They were negotiating the final price while Payal had just finished bargaining with a shopkeeper selling ivory bangles.

'You're making a big mistake, Chandni. Bhaskaran is impotent,' Payal warned.

Chandni looked at Bhaskaran who shivered at the allegation. 'I swear I never crossed any limits in life,' he clarified.

Chandni winked at Payal. 'I know he's not impotent,' she smiled. All the girls laughed in unison.

'What about Reshma?' Som whispered to Bhaskaran.

'What about her?' Bhaskaran was now angry. 'I just saw her nude in the bathroom by accident, OK? Now please hang me for it, you prude!'

Meanwhile, Raja Ghoshal was trying to strike up a polite conversation with Payal. 'Get to the point, you fool,' Payal thought.

Basu nudged Garima, 'Finally, our friends Chandni and Som are getting married at Kalighat. Except they are not marrying each other. What was the fun in our arranged marriage? I always wanted to run away from your father!'

'Very funny!' retorted Garima.

At Behala, Ram and Savita were frantically searching for Som and, at Tollygunj, Biswajeet Roy was baying for Bhaskaran's blood.

IN DELHI, TANYA'S mother was being comforted by her brother Rajat Ahluwalia.

'If you know that the boy is good, why should you even bother about his family and region, *jiji*? I know Tanya is not a girl to marry the wrong boy,' he reasoned.

'I have lost all love for Bengalis,' said his sister. 'Banerjee or Mukherjee, they are all the same to me now,' she moaned.

'What's the boy's name by the way?' Rajat asked.

'Som ... Somashish Mukherjee,' Mrs Sachdev said in a laboured voice.

The name rang a bell somewhere in Rajat's mind. After a brief struggle, realisation dawned upon him.

'If this is the same boy who wrote the best copy test I've ever seen, then congratulations, jiji. Stop crying now,' laughed Rajat.

If words could kill, Biswajeet Roy and Ram Mukherjee would have assasinated each other had Dr Pandey not arrived on time.

'What are you two fighting over? The marriages have happened. You can't undo anything now,' Dr Pandey thundered.

Everybody was silent.

Savita was distraught and pale. Rahul looked mortally scared. He had just returned in the morning from a college trip to Darjeeling only to find total acrimony in the house.

'Listen gentlemen, the boys had very valid reasons,' defended Dr Pandey. 'Mr Roy, why should you play God with Chandni's life just because you brought her to the world? Bhaskaran was your choice and he had no demands whatsoever.'

He then turned towards Ram. 'Mr Mukherjee, Som and Tanya fell in love even before they could realise it. In fact, they were as good as married, if you know what I mean. But Som didn't have the guts to tell you that he loved a Punjabi girl.'

Ram Mukherjee contested the professor's view. 'None of the boys are even settled, Dr Pandey. How will they even run their households?'

'That's not true,' replied Dr Pandey.

'EPP Public Affairs has refused to sell one per cent stake to us. But they are acquiring One Up Masters for two crore Indian rupees. Not only this, every staff member will now be an employee of EPP and both Som and Bhaskaran will sit in their Asia Pacific management board as managing partners,' he revealed.

'Since all of us who invested money have doubled their returns in this deal, I am gifting half my share to Som and Tanya. Som will have thirty lakh to buy a house after you have deducted your five lakh, Ram Babu! And Mr Roy, Bhaskaran now has sixty lakh as spare funds, slightly less than what he was paid by Saklani, but enough to bail you out with a soft loan. And both the boys have careers that many forty-year-olds would die for,' Dr Pandey added for emphasis.

The two Bengali men stood speechless.

Savita blurted out, '*Ami to Somke bokini*. I only asked him why he tried to deceive me by passing off *Taniiaa* as Tanu.'

Heavy footfalls interrupted the conversation.

'No, Ma. I always call her Tanu,' Som led the marriage party into the living room.

Tears and embraces later, all was forgiven and forgotten.

In the evening, the new daughters-in-law showcased their skills over heaps of rasogollas and sandesh. Garima, along with Tanya, now Tanu, sang *Garjat barsat saawan aayo* re and Chandni danced around with the grace of a peacock.

Afterwards, it was one happy story.

Som had emerged victorious from the soup he had landed in. But there were some key messages for everyone. Chandni, for one, learnt to follow her heart. Bhaskaran too learnt to use his heart more than his head.

Tanya now knew that sulking in silence doesn't pay. For Som, it was the lesson of a lifetime – to stand up and fight for what duly belongs to one.

The biggest message, however, was for Saklani.

True acquisitions, he learnt, went beyond just balance sheets.